If this were a date, *Acey thought,* this would be the moment I kiss Harry.

Acey, her mind chastised, *kissing and related activities are not part of the plan. The plan is the priority. Follow through.*

She forced herself to smile with her own lips stretched thin, tight and unapproachable. Very difficult, considering that her libido was screaming at her to do the opposite.

Acey was fast realizing that being with Harry was becoming more and more of a challenge. She was going to have to kick it up a notch. Maybe more for her sake than his, at this point. She feared losing her senses if she hung around him much longer. She was going to fast-track him to that money, so she could fast-track herself away from him. Acey lifted her chin in resolution.

Harry Wells was about to get a healthy dose of tough love.

Love?

Dear Reader,

It's hot and sunny in my neck of the woods—in other words, perfect beach reading weather! And we at Silhouette Special Edition are thrilled to start off your month with the long-awaited new book in *New York Times* bestselling author Debbie Macomber's Navy series, *Navy Husband.* It features a single widowed mother; her naval-phobic sister, assigned to care for her niece while her sister is in the service; and a handsome lieutenant commander who won't take no for an answer! In this case, I definitely think you'll find this book worth the wait....

Next, we begin our new inline series, MOST LIKELY TO..., the story of a college reunion and the about-to-be-revealed secret that is going to change everyone's lives. In *The Homecoming Hero Returns* by Joan Elliott Pickart, a young man once poised for athletic stardom who chose marriage and fatherhood instead finds himself face-to-face with the road not taken. In Stella Bagwell's next book in her MEN OF THE WEST series, *Redwing's Lady,* a Native American deputy sheriff and a single mother learn they have more in common than they thought. *The Father Factor* by Lilian Darcy tells the story of the reunion between a hotshot big-city corporate lawyer who's about to discover the truth about his father—and a woman with a secret of her own. If you've ever bought a lottery ticket, wondering, if just once, it could be possible...be sure to grab *Ticket to Love* by Jen Safrey, in which a pizza waitress from Long Island is sure that if *she* isn't the lucky winner, it must be the handsome stranger in town. Last, new-to-Silhouette author Jessica Bird begins THE MOOREHOUSE LEGACY, a miniseries based on three siblings who own an upstate New York inn, with *Beauty and the Black Sheep.* In it, responsible sister Frankie Moorehouse wonders if just this once she could think of herself first as soon as she lays eyes on her temporary new chef.

So keep reading! And think of us as the dog days of August begin to set in....

Toodles,

Gail Chasan
Senior Editor

JEN SAFREY

TICKET TO LOVE

Silhouette®

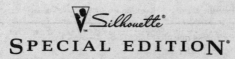

SPECIAL EDITION®

Published by Silhouette Books

America's Publisher of Contemporary Romance

This book is for New York, a city powered by millions of dreams. And I especially dedicate this book to Valley Stream. I've noticed most people have a love-hate relationship with where they grew up. This book was written in my moments of love.

SILHOUETTE BOOKS

ISBN 0-373-24697-8

TICKET TO LOVE

This edition published by arrangement with Harlequin Books S.A.

Visit Silhouette Books at www.eHarlequin.com

Printed in U.S.A.

Books by Jen Safrey

Silhouette Special Edition

A Perfect Pair #1590
Ticket to Love #1697

JEN SAFREY

grew up in Valley Stream, New York, and graduated from Boston University in 1993. She is a nearly ten-year veteran of the news copy desk at the *Boston Herald.* Past and present, she has been a champion baton twirler, an accomplished flutist, an equestrienne, a student of ashtanga yoga and a belly dancer. Jen would love to hear from readers at jen02106@lycos.com.

Milk, Juice, Eggs…Jackpot?

You'd better believe it, readers—some lucky person picked up more than pantry staples at the Bread and Milk bodega right here in Valley Stream, Long Island. Last night, the New York Lottery picked a winner for the $35 million-dollar jackpot. That ticket was sold by the owner of this humble neighborhood grocery, who hopes that this news will be good for her business.

Unfortunately, the *Post* is unable to reveal the identity of the winner. That's right, *winner*—lottery officials determine that only *one* winning ticket was sold. So be kind to your neighbors, because you *could* be talking to a brand-new millionaire!

Chapter One

"Aaahhh!"

A piercing, someone-is-being-ax-murdered scream shattered the early-evening peace in the apartment Acey shared with her younger sister.

"Yeow!"

A startled Acey accidentally pressed her scalding curling iron against her cheek. "Damn!" she said. She tried to untangle a lock of long thick black hair from the contraption. "Stephanie! Are you all right?" she called.

"Acey!" Steph screamed. "Get in here! Quick! Fast!"

Between Steph's shrieks, the smell of scorching hair ends and the rising red blotch on her cheek, Acey was getting agitated. Steph was even-keeled, polite, quiet. Acey knew the one prone to the trademark Corelli excitement and hissy fits was herself. It was disconcerting, to say the absolute least, to hear Steph screaming like a banshee.

Acey finally dropped the hot iron onto the bathroom countertop and fled down the short hallway as Steph kept screaming. "Acey! Acey!"

Acey screeched to a halt in the small living room, where Steph was standing in front of the television, hands now covering her mouth in disbelief. "What? What is it?" Acey demanded.

Steph pointed at the TV, which was showing a picture of Bread and Milk, the convenience store two blocks away where the sisters constantly ran for food-and-drink emergencies. Acey shook her head, not understanding. Steph turned up the volume just as the reporter thrust a microphone into the face of Rosalia, the store's owner. Acey panicked a moment at the sight of one of her favorite people on the news.

"Is she okay?" Acey asked, then realized she should just listen.

"Yes, we're very excited," Rosalia was saying in her Colombian accent, still thick despite her many years just outside New York City. "It's a very good thing for our store."

The camera cut away and Acey yelled, "*What?* What's a good thing?" Then a series of numbers flashed against a blue background. "These are the numbers," the anchorwoman trilled, "that are worth thirty-five million dollars. So if you are a Bread and Milk customer and haven't taken a good look at that ticket you bought yesterday, now might be the time." Then she turned to the meteorologist and asked him for the weekend forecast.

Steph was scratching the numbers into the notebook she always kept handy, then muted the television. The sisters stared at each other.

"Did I hear that right?" Acey asked quietly.

"They picked the thirty-five-million-dollar numbers in the New York lottery last night," Steph said. "There was one winner. One winning ticket. And it was bought at our store."

Neither woman moved. Acey could tell from her sister's wide-eyed expression that they were thinking the same thing. They talked about it every week when they cashed their meager paychecks up the street. They talked about it every month when they had to decide which bill was going to have to be paid late.

It shimmered in the air there between them, dancing for them, teasing them that it could be real.

Both women bolted.

They flew down the hall and reached their bedroom doorway simultaneously, smashing into each other and crushing through together, each wanting to be the first to touch the ticket. They flung themselves at the dresser, and the mirror on top shimmied precariously. They both frantically searched the top of the dresser but came up empty.

"Where is it?" Steph shouted.

"I always put it here! Right here!" Acey cried in a panic. She picked up various porcelain trinket boxes, shaking the cheap gold-plated chains inside, finding nothing but a thin layer of dust under each one. "Where is it? Where is it?"

"We *did* buy one yesterday, right?"

"We have not forgotten one Thursday since you were legally old enough to go halves with me. And you were with me when I bought it yesterday, remember? They had no lemon Snapple and you had to get raspberry?"

"Check your purse!" Steph screamed. "Check your pockets! Check everything!"

Acey was distracted by her sister's histrionics. For the first time, Steph seemed to be able to outfreak Acey herself. It was like long-awaited proof that she was a Corelli, too.

Acey leaped onto her bed and dumped the contents of her purse. She rifled through gum wrappers and uncapped pens and ATM receipts. Steph was flinging clothes out of the laundry hamper, searching, Acey guessed, for the jeans she'd worn yesterday. Acey flipped open her wallet and pulled out the only two dollars in there, then held the wallet upside down, willing something she couldn't see to magically fall out of it.

When it didn't, she began to wail. "It can't be missing, it just can't, it can't..."

"Keep looking!" Steph barked, thrusting her hands into denim pockets. "Don't stop. Just shut up until you find it!"

The next twenty minutes were a blur. Acey and Steph were driven to turning over sofa cushions and searching in unthinkable places like the freezer and the mailbox. Acey could hear her sister chanting softly, "Thirty-five million, thirty-five million," and Acey's own heart felt as if it might stop.

If only they didn't do Quick Picks all the time. If she and Steph had played their own numbers, they'd have known right away if it was necessary to rip the apartment to shreds. But maybe they had hit, and it was gone, gone...

No. She couldn't freak out. Steph would kill her. Of course, if they didn't find the ticket, it was highly likely Steph would kill her anyway, but… Acey lifted the lumpy braided throw rug, and their cat, Sherlock, darted out from underneath it. He glared at Acey with affront, then raised his back leg and licked himself. "Sherlock," Acey said, "the cat without a clue."

Sherlock stopped licking and looked glad he couldn't understand English because he suspected he was being insulted. "I wish we had a dog," Acey said through gritted teeth, replacing the rug. "A bloodhound. So it could help us. But, no. All *you* do is nap and play with—" Paper!

Acey ran to her sister, who was emptying the silverware drawer. "Steph, you're the mystery writer. Solve this case. It involves a cat who loves to play with little bits of paper."

Steph dropped a handful of forks and streaked back into the bedroom, Acey on her heels, until she got to Sherlock's cat bed, between the girls' beds. And there, in the center, was the ticket. Acey and Steph moved toward it with a reverence reserved for the Holy Grail. And just as Acey was lowering her hand toward the hair-covered cushion, from out of nowhere Sherlock bounced off a bed and landed on the ticket.

"No!" Acey whispered.

Sherlock, apparently in revenge for Acey's sarcasm two moments prior, clamped down on the ticket with his teeth.

Steph grabbed Sherlock's feather toy, which was lying nearby. She shook it, and Sherlock was distracted, mesmerized by the motion and the little tinkly bell. He dropped the ticket. In slow motion, Acey crept her hand toward him, and had one finger on the ticket when she got scratched.

"Ow!" she said, pulling back her freshly bleeding hand. Sherlock circled once and sat on the ticket.

Steph, still on her hands and knees, crawled behind Sherlock and lifted him up. Acey reached again for the ticket, crooning, "Nice kitty, nice kitty," and pulled her hand away before the next swipe could get her. Steph adjusted her hold on the cat so both his front legs were spread wide. He wriggled, but not quickly enough. Acey had it in her hand.

Jackpot.

Steph lowered Sherlock, and she and Acey stared down at the ticket, which was a bit wrinkled but miraculously had no punctures.

"Go get the numbers," Acey finally said. "I'll check the date and make sure it's the right ticket."

Steph scampered off. In Acey's palm, the ticket felt heavier than a piece of paper, and her hand shook with exhaustion and anticipation. She found yesterday's date—May 24—and took a deep breath. Steph stepped back into the room and Acey saw her steady herself.

"Ready?" Steph asked.

"Ready." Acey squeezed her eyes shut.

"All right. Here I go. The first number is…four."

Acey opened her eyes and looked at the first number on the ticket.

Eight.

"Argh!" She threw the ticket as hard as she could. Being paper, it just floated to the floor at her feet. Acey stomped on it. "I can't believe it! After all that!"

Steph picked up the ticket and checked the numbers

against her notebook. "Sheesh. We didn't even get *one* number."

Acey flopped onto her bed as dramatically as she knew how. "In twenty-seven whole years on this planet, *why* can't anything good happen to *me? Ever?*"

"Join the club."

Acey shook her head. "No. Everything I try goes to hell. At least you're writing books." In fact, that was why Steph had caught the lottery story. She religiously parked herself in front of the news every single night when she got back from her receptionist's job at the local hair salon. She considered the news a treasure trove of ideas for the mystery novels she'd been writing since she was about fifteen. Acey was jealous of her smart, two-years-younger sister sometimes, knowing deep down that if one of them was going to be successful, it wouldn't be Acey.

"I'm writing books, but I'm not *selling* books. I got another rejection letter two days ago."

"So what? At least you're *doing* something. I'm doomed to struggle every day at the pizza place for the rest of my life."

"Acey, there are a million things you could do if you really wanted to. You always make all these plans and then you never follow through. Maybe you could—"

"If you don't mind, I don't want to talk about my dim future. I'd rather dwell on the deep disappointment of not winning thirty-five million."

"If it makes you feel any better, you would have had to give me half."

Acey sighed loudly.

Steph went to sit down on her bed, but the contents

of two dresser drawers were piled there, so she nudged Acey over and sat down next to her. Now that the craziness had passed, Acey noticed, Steph was back to her calm, rational self. "Listen," Steph said, "it's not as if we expect to win when we buy lottery tickets. Not really. It's just a dream."

"But I thought it was us just now, finally. Didn't you think it was us?"

Steph lay down. "Yeah. I thought it was us."

Acey stayed silent for a few minutes, her heartbeat slowing from thumping to unnoticeable. "If we'd won, we could have hired a maid to clean all this up. Now *we're* stuck doing it."

Steph chuckled. "Let's just be glad Ma and Dad are in Florida now. The sight of this place now would kill her."

Acey smiled. "'Annamaria Christina Corelli!'" she mimicked. "'This place is a disaster!' But, Ma, it's Steph's fault. 'Stephanie Cara Corelli!'" Acey giggled. "Like our full names are supposed to scare us into picking things up."

"My name did scare me in kindergarten," Steph said. "Too many letters to learn to write."

"At least Dad made it easier for me," Acey said. It was true. Daunted by his elder daughter's mouthful of a name, and perhaps with a part of him longing for a son, he nicknamed her A.C. Many years of her parents' shouting it up the stairs had morphed it into Acey.

Acey grinned, but remembered a moment later that this was a somber occasion. Stretching her arms over her head, she said, "Well, whoever won, it's still pretty cool that it's one of us. Someone who lives here in Valley Stream."

"Could be anyone. Could be an out-of-towner."

"No," Acey said. A plane passed low over their building, and she listened until she couldn't hear it anymore before adding, "I just have a feeling it's a neighbor. Someone like us. Someone who works hard and who's probably kind of nice."

"That does make sense. Bread and Milk isn't exactly a tourist attraction. It's probably someone we see in there all the time."

"But who?" Acey tried to conjure up memories of anyone she'd ever noticed in there. The idea that the future millionaire had walked among them left Acey flummoxed. "Wow, I'm dying to know who it is now."

"Maybe you'll have to wait," Steph said. "It was just last night, after all."

"True. No one with thirty-five million dollars is going to just want to keep living a boring old life around here." Acey sighed. "No one."

Harry unwrapped his Italian hero and regarded it with love as it sat in its white paper nest. Salami pieces and shreds of provolone had fallen out of the thick sandwich, and oil was forming a little puddle around it. It was one of the most beautiful things he'd ever seen, and he'd just about seen it all.

Whenever a little corner of his heart began to yearn for his Texas life, whenever a section of his brain began to wonder if leaving behind everything he knew and coming to New York wasn't a lunatic idea, Harry just went out and found himself a sandwich. New York tasted better than any place he'd ever been.

He hefted the huge hero to his face and his biceps

actually strained. He inhaled the scent of the oil. Ah. He opened his mouth and took a tremendous bite of his new life. Oil dribbled down his chin. He grabbed one of the fifty-seven napkins the deli guy had tossed into his bag, wiped his face and picked up the remote. He flipped around before deciding on the local news.

He dived into his sandwich again and looked over it to numbers blinking at him from the TV screen. "These are the numbers," the anchorwoman was saying, "that are worth thirty-five million dollars. So if you are a Bread and Milk customer and haven't taken a good look at that ticket you bought yesterday, now might be the time."

Harry ceased chewing, and the food just floated around his mouth as he sat, frozen. He felt something greasy run down his hand into his sleeve, but still he didn't move.

Something about the newswoman's voice. So happy. Delighted to be reporting what everyone must consider good news. Someone who wasn't a millionaire yesterday is a millionaire today.

He looked at her smiling plastic face, now listening to the weatherman saying something about a warming trend. *She doesn't think at all that she just delivered the worst news of the day,* Harry thought. The newscast before this story was undoubtedly filled with fires and famine, wars and woes. Clearly, they'd saved the "happy" story until the end.

Harry dropped the sandwich back onto the paper on the coffee table in front of him and sat back. He knew, knew for a sad fact, that the person with the winning ticket was the unluckiest person who ever lived. He, or she, didn't know it now, and they wouldn't know it when they were cut a nice big check, and they wouldn't know it when they bought their new enormous mansion in Beverly Hills or the Hamptons or in the south of France. But slowly, over time, the money, the privilege, would turn them into something else, something not even human, something that was a danger to others.

Harry's left leg twinged, and he glanced down at it. Encased in jeans, ending in a sharply pointed cowboy boot, it looked like any other leg. If he took off the denim, and peeled off skin, he knew he'd see an abnormality—a steel pin, the best money could buy, which was ironic since money was what sent him to the operating room in the first place.

He hated when he remembered. He tried not to remember, ever, but the littlest thing could set it off—a person at the bus stop on crutches, or a horse-race recap show on cable. Then his mind swirled him away from his living room or the street or wherever he was, and threw him back under his horse, the animal writhing and crying out in ceaseless pain, crushing Harry's bones as it struggled and failed to get up.

Money, the bottomless money that was his birthright, the money he had tossed around full-time on ski slopes and cliff edges, had eventually ended the life of a beautiful animal. Lying in a hospital bed, reading a magazine account of those awful moments, Harry had wished it had ended his own, too.

Harry bolted up from the sofa and lurched into the kitchen, weighted down by his own memories. He stood in front of the refrigerator and there, under a magnet among photos of his sisters, was yesterday's lottery ticket. He'd never bought a lottery ticket in his life. He'd even laughed a little bit at the irony while standing in line at Bread and Milk. But he'd wanted to pick one up for Joe, his downstairs neighbor, who was in Boston this week visiting his daughter. Joe had spent the better part of last weekend helping Harry fix his air conditioner. He'd refused payment so Harry, knowing Joe religiously played the lottery, figured the least he could do was offer to pick him up a ticket. "I'd appreciate it, man," Joe had said with a grin. "I'll throw you a couple mil if I hit." Harry had winced at the irony—he could've thrown Joe a couple mil any day of the week. But he bought the ticket.

He looked at it now. The first number was eleven. He remembered a four on the television. So that was that.

The eleven seemed to stare back at him. One-one. Like two people, two identical people, standing side by side. Like Harry and the new millionaire. One person nearly destroyed, and one person about to be. Harry slid the ticket out from under the magnet and went to toss it in the trash, but for some reason, he couldn't let it drop out of his hand. Instead, he just folded it over so he didn't have to see the eleven, or any of the other numbers, and tacked it back up to the fridge. He opened the fridge, grabbed a can of root beer and carried it back to the living room.

His sandwich was there, at least as appetizing as before. His life here was okay. He could handle an occasional reminder, as long as he didn't dwell on it, he told himself. He grabbed the remote and changed the channel, and found talk of the lottery on the competing news station.

"I can't wait to see who it is," this woman was bubbling to her coanchor.

"I can," Harry told her, picking up his hero again. "That poor, unlucky slob."

Chapter Two

Acey was late for work, which was why she was running.

Acey loved her cute little slide-on white sneakers, which was why she was wearing them.

But her cute little sneakers were not meant for running, which was why, halfway to work, she fell.

She picked herself up from her sprawl across the hard, scratchy sidewalk, wincing. She examined her knee, now dirty with a thin rivulet of blood trickling down her calf.

"Are you all right?" she heard a man ask behind her.

"Oh, yeah, I just love falling on my butt in pub—" she raised her head and looked up at the man "—lic."

"Don't worry, it's hardly public," the man said. "No one's around. Can you stand?"

I'm not sure, she thought. If she had already been

standing, she would have gone weak in the knees with one look at this guy.

His hair was—well, she would have guessed light brown, but a bit of angling sunlight lightened it to the color of Long Island's South Shore sand. The short strands were silky. Acey wished she knew what shampoo he used. His chin appeared chiseled from Italian marble and his lips were curved in a wide smile. His eyes were blue. Very blue. Bluer than the bluest crayon she and Steph had ever fought over, and his long, long eyelashes curled away from his profile.

"I can stand. I didn't break anything. Just skin," she finally said. The man took her hand, which was shaking a little bit, as she rose to her feet. She winced again. "Oh, it stings. I hate these sneakers. They always make me trip."

"Why do you wear them, then?"

"Because," she said, smoothing down her top, "they're cute."

"Ah."

"But now they're filling up with blood, which isn't very cute."

"Listen, come into my apartment. You can wash your knee and bandage it up."

Come into his apartment? Oh, no. She'd learned a thing or two watching the news with Steph.

"No, thanks, but I can't," she said. "I'm late."

"You'll be really late," he drawled, "if you lose all your blood before you get there."

"That wouldn't happen." But Acey, despite her reservations, was having a hard time turning and limping away. She lingered. "I shouldn't be talking to a stranger anyway." She couldn't help teasing, late or not. "Not just a stranger to me, but to this state, I bet. Southern?"

"Texas."

"Uh-huh," Acey said, thinking. "Well, I do like steak. And sometimes I catch the rodeo stuff on cable. You do that kind of thing?"

He appeared to be holding back a grin. "Not really."

"Too bad. It looks cool. Been here long?"

"A few months."

"Why Valley Stream?"

"Why not?"

She nodded. "Why aren't you at work?"

"I work from home."

"Doing…?"

"Grant writing."

"What's your name?"

"Harry."

"Last name?"

"Wells. Is the interview about over? I think it's time to clean your knee."

"I guess it's all right." She extended her right hand. "I'm Acey Corelli."

"Interesting name."

"I'm an interesting person." Harry stared at her, and Acey blushed. He took her elbow.

"Go on ahead, Acey. The door's open."

She took one step and stopped. "Just so you know, I'm not that kind of girl. I don't just meet men and get myself invited in. It's only because I'm a…a damsel in distress right now. And you seem to be a genuine Southern gentleman."

Harry was charmed. "I am. And your self-analysis is duly noted."

"Okay, then."

She walked ahead of him to his door, and Harry forced

himself to look at the back of her head so he wouldn't look at her…oh, forget it. No use fighting biology.

"It's open," he said again, and Acey pushed through the door. She leaned against it so he could pass through, and then she followed him up to his apartment. Harry said, "The bathroom is that way. I'll show you."

"I'll find it," Acey said, her tone implying she didn't need any nursing, and left the room. "Where are the Band-Aids?" she called a second later.

"Cabinet above the sink."

"Anything in there that might scare me?"

Harry thought for a moment, decided the athlete's-foot cream wouldn't be too disconcerting, and answered, "No."

He heard the bathroom door close, and he leaned against his table. This was a little strange. He'd never had a woman here, in this apartment, before. He wandered into the living room.

The water shut off and, almost immediately, Acey emerged. Her knee was covered with two crossing Band-Aids, marring the perfect landscape of her leg. She smiled, and said, "Nice place you got here. It's, well, it's really clean. A hospital's not even this clean."

Harry laughed. "Clean" was pretty much the only thing you could say about it. It was devoid of decoration, a purely functional white-walled enclosure. Thanks to the influence of many maids in his mother's employ, Harry was only happy in sterile surroundings. "I don't really like a lot of clutter. Or even a little clutter."

"That's all right. I'm not criticizing, just curious." She shifted her feet, a bit uneasy. Harry knew he was capable of putting her at ease with a gesture, a conversation starter, a drink. He'd done it a hundred times in his life. But he just couldn't right now.

Another two beats went by. "Well," Acey said, "I really should be on my way." She glanced at her watch, perhaps just as an excuse, but then her eyes opened very wide. "Oh, crap, I *really* should be on my way." She practically ran to the front door. "This was very decent of you, cowboy. Thanks. See you around."

Harry fumbled for something to say, but before he could, Acey Corelli winked and was out the door even faster than she'd literally fallen into his life. The strange thing was, he already missed her.

"Sicilian pie, peppers and mushrooms!" Acey shouted over her shoulder while adding up the total on the register. She waited for a middle-aged woman to count the money out of her wallet and took stock of the now-empty restaurant. The lunch crowd started before eleven on weekdays, and the time always flew by until two, leaving Acey with her face and neck sweating from the ovens.

"Sicilian, peppers and mushrooms," Anthony repeated, sliding the pizza onto the counter. Acey folded the cardboard box like an origami expert and placed the pie inside. "Thanks for coming to Focaccia's," she said to the customer.

No one else stepped up to the counter. Acey could actually hear herself think again, and could now hear the piped-in easy-listening music. Acey sang with Carole King as she threw a rag down on the counter and wiped it clean.

"Come on, Lydia, for God's sake," Acey heard behind her, and rolled her eyes. *Here we go again,* she thought. Anthony and Lydia were like a broken record.

"Shut up," Lydia said, then stomped over to Acey. Her bleached-blond hair was in a neat, sleek ponytail. "Acey, tell that gorilla I hate him. And we're never speaking again."

Since Lydia was clearly relying on her as a fellow woman, Acey at least tried to be tactful. "Um, you both work here. I don't think you can get away with not talking."

"I'd rather quit than work with that…that…"

"So, why don't you?" Acey asked, knowing the answer never changed but also knowing she was expected to show interest every time drama arose.

"*He* should be the one quitting," Lydia said. "*My* father owns this place."

"I don't think he's quitting." Acey patted Lydia's shoulder and Lydia grabbed Acey's hand.

"Hon, that's a nice set of tips. Look at that color." Acey grinned. No Long Island girl worth her salt went without fake nails. They were a bit of an expense, but Steph worked at a salon, so Acey got a good deal. Lydia examined the little rhinestones and said, "He's such a Scorpio. He'll never change."

So much for getting her off the topic. "You know," Acey said, "I think you two are the perfect couple. So you fight—" all the time "—but everyone fights. I heard that the couples who fight the worst are the ones most in love. Because they know how to push each other's buttons."

"Who said that? Dr. Phil?"

"I don't remember. Maybe. Just be nice to him. I know he loves you." This was true. As often as they argued, Anthony was always doing nice things for Lydia. Buying her little gold charms, taking her bowling even though he hated it, bringing her flowers. Acey thought they were the nicest couple, *when* they were being nice. Their fights were only over stupid things, but they escalated because they both enjoyed yelling.

"Yeah," Anthony said, coming around behind Acey and giving her a platonic kiss on the cheek. "Thanks, babe." He glanced at the sulking Lydia. "You should listen to your friend here. I'm a good guy."

"Please. I wouldn't come back to you if *you* were the lottery winner."

"That's interesting, huh?" Anthony said. "No one came forward yet."

"Nope," Acey said. She'd planted herself in front of the news every night for almost a full week with Steph, but no word. That no winner had revealed himself was becoming more of a story than the fact that there was a winner.

"What kind of a moron doesn't take the money?" Lydia asked. "I'd *run* to the lottery office."

"Maybe someone who's out of the country. Doesn't know he won," Anthony said.

"Or maybe someone who doesn't speak English, and didn't hear it on the news," Lydia suggested, temporarily forgetting the silent treatment.

Acey didn't remind her. "Maybe the winner is scared." This was her new theory, after discussing it last night with Steph.

"Scared? Of what? Being rich?" Anthony laughed.

Two junior-high-age boys approached the counter and asked Acey for *zeppoles*. She submerged five dough balls in the deep fryer. Lydia was saying, "It's true. Like, if you've been dirt-poor your whole life, suddenly having all that money would be a jolt to your system."

"I'm sure *I* could handle it," Anthony replied. "Besides, I don't think anyone around here is dirt-poor. Just average."

Acey lifted the crispy *zeppoles* from the fryer, dropped them into a brown paper bag, and sprinkled in a generous amount of powdered sugar. She folded the top of the bag and shook vigorously, then handed it to one of the boys. Taking their money, she asked, "Shouldn't you be in school?"

Both boys looked supremely guilty.

"Next time you come in here during school hours, I'm going to charge you double. Got it?" she said. The pair scampered off.

"What about you, Acey?" Lydia asked.

"What about me?" Acey wiped her hands on her filthy white apron.

"Would you take the thirty-five million dollars in one lump sum, or the yearly checks?"

Acey considered a moment. "Yearly checks. That way, you'd always have a little something to look forward to. Or, a big something."

"Not me," Anthony said. "I'd take one payment. That way, if I ever got hit by a bus or whatever, my family would have the money right away."

"If *only* you'd get hit by a bus," Lydia muttered, and Anthony smiled as if she'd said something quite sweet.

"Anyway," Acey interjected before any more yelling could commence, "I'm really dying to know who it is. Aren't you guys?"

"No," Lydia said, staring out the window at the busy avenue. "All I know is, it isn't me."

"I don't care," Anthony said. "Winning would be great, but I got something worth more than a lousy thirty-five million."

Lydia looked back at him, and he winked at her. She threw herself into his arms, nearly knocking him backward. "You're worth a hundred million," she mumbled, kissing his mouth.

"You're worth a *million* million."

She pushed him against the counter, grabbed the back of his head and kissed him even more deeply.

"Guys, seriously," Acey said, "take it to the back. People are coming in."

The lovers stumbled together toward the restrooms, pressed together and running their hands all over each other. Acey fanned herself with one hand.

It had been so long since she'd had any kind of feeling for any man. Charlie had been the last, and after the way he and his family had treated her, it was easy to never want to have those feelings again. In fact, the first time she'd since felt any real stirrings was today, with that cowboy. And those had been the most genuine stirrings she'd *ever* felt. Too bad she hadn't had time to do some more flirting. Well, he lived in the neighborhood now. She was sure fate would put him in her path again.

Acey stepped up to the counter and cut slices to order from the ready-made pies. But she took a second to peer once more at Romeo and Juliet in the back, and she knew that she, too, would rather have someone to love than a million million.

When Steve showed up to relieve Acey at seven, she scrunched up her greasy apron, tossed it in the employees' coatroom and, with one wave over her shoulder, strolled out of Focaccia's. Usually the walk home took her fifteen minutes, but today she was detouring around the corner.

Right through Bread and Milk.

Her week-old curiosity had nearly killed her, but now it was time for action.

Acey peeled off her denim jacket as she walked. The last couple of days had been unseasonably chilly and rainy, but now that June was here, it seemed the weather had decided to cooperate with the calendar.

She turned a corner, stopped and regarded Bread and Milk from across the street. There were haphazard signs in the window for sales and specials, and one was misspelled. "Corn mufins, 75 cents." It wasn't unusual, but this neighborhood didn't care. Rosalia's store was open from six in the morning until eleven at night, and Rosalia herself was almost always in the store.

Bread and Milk seemed to sparkle a bit now that it had sold the winning lottery ticket. Acey crossed the street. The door was propped open and no one was behind the counter. Acey wandered over to the refrigerator case and grabbed a carton of orange juice. Rosalia came out from her stockroom, hauling a box that had to be twice as heavy as she was.

"Hi!" Acey cried, putting the orange juice on the front counter and rushing over to take the box from her friend.

"Oh, Acey, don't do that," Rosalia scolded, but Acey ignored her and took the box, straining to hold it straight.

"Where does this go?"

"By the register there. You're so sweet."

"No problem," Acey said. She dropped the box where Rosalia had indicated—really dropped, when it slipped out of her fingers—but she didn't hear anything break. She turned to Rosalia and flexed a bicep. "Strong, huh? Check that out."

Rosalia laughed. "Stronger than my boys. Wish you worked here and not my no-good bums."

"I'd love to work here," Acey said, and it was true. It was a friendly store, where everyone said hello and made small talk, and it was a thousand times quieter, without the soap operas that went on at Focaccia's.

Rosalia put her hands on her hips and shook her head. Rosalia had a way about her, a way of carrying herself that made Acey ashamed of her own slumping. Rosalia was at least five foot ten, and walked with the book-balancing poise of a Miss Colombia. Her still-long hair was graying with middle age, but it looked so fashionable on her that Acey was sure she inspired other approaching-senior-age female customers to follow suit. Her clothes were nondescript sweatshirts and jeans, but Acey thought that even if she dressed in the trendiest fashions, no one would notice them once she flashed her always-lipsticked smile.

"Haven't seen you in a while, Acey."

"Oh, but I've seen *you!* On TV, eh?"

Rosalia tried to appear nonchalant, but her grin was an easy giveaway. "Just lucky. Really. You won't believe how lucky."

"Sure I'd believe it. The store gets a nice cut, right?"

"I'll get what's coming to me, yes." Rosalia moved to the other side of the counter and rang up the juice.

Acey slid the top half of her body across the counter with her money and lowered her voice. "Tell me. Do you know who it is? Who won?"

"No one knows, huh?"

"No, not officially, but..." A man plopped two rolls of toilet paper on the counter and asked for cigarettes. Acey stepped aside until his purchases were bagged and he was on his way. Then she leaned in again. "You must have some idea who won, Rosalia."

"Why you say that?"

"Because you know just about every single customer by name around here. Did someone tell you? Tell me. I'll keep it a secret, I swear."

"I bet."

"I will!" Acey protested, but Rosalia's eyes were sparkling. "Come on. Spill it."

"I don't have anything to tell you. Still a mystery."

With one last scrutinizing gaze at Rosalia's face to see if she was holding out, Acey slumped her shoulders. "I was so certain you'd know."

"I am surprised, it's true," Rosalia said, smoothing a strand of hair behind her ear. "If someone win, I think they would come in here and be—" she waved her arms around "—woooo…"

"Exactly. But no?"

"No. It is a mystery," Rosalia repeated.

Acey picked up her plastic bag. "Oh, well. I guess I'll just keep wondering."

She took one step toward the door and was about to say goodbye when Rosalia said quietly, "But."

Acey whirled around.

"I am thinking someone."

Acey rushed back and dropped her bag on the floor. "Aha! You *do* have a suspect!"

"I know nothing," Rosalia said in a stern mother's voice. "I am only thinking."

Acey circled her hand in an impatient "go on" gesture.

"There is a man. He started coming in here maybe six months ago. About your age. Not from here."

"He has an accent?"

"Yes. And so nice. He asks about my daughter's daughter all the time after he once seen them here. And in February, that big snow, he shoveled the front for me. He helps me, like you do."

"What's his name?"

"I don't know. He asks about me but keeps so silent about him. But he, he bought a ticket that day. For some reason, I think…everyone else would come tell me if they win but he's so quiet, maybe he's keeping quiet on that, too."

Acey thought a moment. "Has he been in here since the numbers were picked?"

"Yes, but he acts the same. Nothing different but I have a feeling about him."

"Huh."

"Maybe," Rosalia said, "you can look at him, tell me if you have the feeling, too? He comes every day, at almost exactly five minutes after one, for lemonade."

"Interesting. Okay," Acey decided. "I'll be here tomorrow at five after one. Just point him out to me."

"You won't miss him," Rosalia said. "I think no girl would miss him."

"You won't even notice I'm gone. Twenty minutes, Lydia, please?"

Acey glanced nervously at the clock. As usual, the time had flown by and it was now five of one.

"Oh, crap, Acey, it's crazy in here," Lydia complained, slicing a pie and boxing it.

"I know, but I have a…a…" Acey struggled. "A doctor's appointment."

"Twenty minutes for a doctor's appointment?"

Acey hated to lie, so she hardly ever did. Which was why she was so awful at it. "They're squeezing me in."

Lydia paused and studied her. Acey squirmed with guilt. Why *was* she doing this anyhow? Wasn't Lydia right yesterday? Why should you care who won the lottery if it wasn't you? But Acey did. For something so wonderful to happen right up the street…it was like a miracle almost, and Acey was a pilgrim. She just wanted the tiniest glimpse at the lucky person. And she desperately wanted it to be someone nice, because people who had piles of money, like Charlie, so often didn't deserve it.

"You never skip out like this," Lydia said. "Is it serious?"

"Um, not really, but like I said, he's fitting me in, so…"

"Are you pregnant?"

Acey handed a customer some change. "Thank you," she said to him. "I'm not even answering that," she said to Lydia.

"Just checking. I mean, I didn't think you've been getting any action since Charlie, but…"

"Can you *please* cover for me?" Acey asked through gritted teeth.

"Well, it's not going to be easy. Okay. I'll do it on one condition."

"Yeah?"

"That you tell me the truth. This is no *doctor* visit. This is about a guy, right?"

The minute hand edged toward one o'clock.

"Yeah," Acey said. "It's about a guy."

"Then go, girl." Lydia grinned. "Twenty minutes."

Acey pulled off her apron. "Can I borrow your sunglasses?"

Lydia pulled them off her head and handed them to Acey, who grabbed them and sprinted out the door.

Acey peeked over a box of Cap'n Crunch and watched the door. She held a shopping basket, but just for show. Lydia's sunglasses were enormous for her face, but they made Acey feel covert. She was on the case. Like Nancy Drew. Nancy Drew with big hair and acrylic nails.

She checked her watch. Four minutes after one.

"It's almost time," she heard in her ear, and jumped about three feet. She turned to find Cassandra, wrapped in her nubby black cardigan, rocking back and forth. "The *end.* It's upon us."

"Oh, okay," Acey said weakly. Cassandra had been a regular for at least a dozen years. Acey didn't know her real name. Steph had nicknamed her Cassandra a long time ago because of her constant doomsday prophesies.

Acey humored Cassandra each time she saw her, which was more and more seldom as the woman aged. The end *was* probably near for her, and it made Acey a little sad. Not for the first time, she wanted to offer Cassandra something, like coffee, but she never knew how to ask so that it sounded more friendly than pitying. The old woman shook her head and shuffled away. Acey sighed, turned back to the cereal and saw that someone had come in. Rosalia was already deep in conversation with him.

Cowboy boots. Really scuffed up, too. As if he'd just left Silver hitched to a mailbox outside.

Acey got a funny little prickly feeling.

Her gaze traveled up long legs. *Long* legs. That

ended in a...wow, nice ass. Much smaller than her own, which usually daunted her but for some reason, she had the urge to slip behind him and see if she could fit that butt in both her cupped hands. Then she could slide one of those hands over his hip and check the size of...

"Oh, my God, Acey," she said out loud. The man looked over his shoulder and Acey dropped to a crouch. She shifted a few boxes of elbow macaroni around so she appeared to be a legitimate shopper. She rose to her feet and peeked at the counter, where Rosalia and the man were chatting again, but now he was leaning one arm on the counter as Rosalia flipped through photos.

It was no shock when Acey saw his face. Harry Wells.

Rosalia glanced up, saw Acey and raised her eyebrows. Acey suspected the thick stack of photos was deliberate on Rosalia's part, to keep their target there long enough for Acey's assessment.

Her assessment? Same as the first time she met him. An Ebert and Roeper two-thumbs-*way*-up.

Being careful to stare at the shelves of sundries, Acey moved up an aisle closer to the front. Yes. Much better. Now she could hear them.

"She's beautiful," Harry was saying.

"She looks just like my daughter," Rosalia said with pride.

"Actually, I see so much of you," Harry answered. "Definitely that smile."

"The *end.*"

Acey realized Cassandra had sneaked up behind the man and repeated her usual proclamation. Harry didn't even seem surprised when he turned around and Cassandra said, "Are you ready? For the end? It's here."

"If the end is truly here, then at least they sent the

most beautiful angel to tell me," he told the soothsayer. Cassandra studied him, nodded, and left the store.

Acey's jaw hung.

"Thank you for showing me your pictures," Harry said to Rosalia. "They really made my day." He grinned. "Now, I guess I should get what I came here for and let y'all get back to work."

Harry took a step in Acey's direction, and her head snapped back around. She pulled open the refrigerator case, yanked out random items and dropped them into her basket. Harry was getting closer, and Acey stared at the floor and silently berated herself. She'd *known* he was coming here for lemonade. Why was she hanging around right *next* to the lemonade? Nancy Drew would have hung her red head in shame.

She peeked over her shoulder and saw Harry go down the next aisle. She dropped the basket and darted for the door before he could see her. She gave Rosalia a hasty wave she hoped her friend would interpret as "talk to you about this later."

She hopped out the door and jumped into the nearest doorway on the left. Mission accomplished. Rosalia wanted her to get a feeling about Harry? She got a feeling, all right. Right down between her thighs. *Damn.*

Her watch said twelve minutes after one. She was about to cross the street to head back to work when she spied the cowboy coming out of Bread and Milk. He was on the opposite corner, walking away from her. And away from Focaccia's.

Acey turned her head toward her place of employment, then walked the other way, following Harry, keeping half a block's distance. Just two minutes. She'd turn back in two minutes.

After about only a minute, Harry ambled up the walkway of his brick apartment building. Acey dashed across the street, tucked herself into the doorway of an orthodontist's office and watched him through the dark glasses. If only she had a good pair of binoculars.

Holy crap. Was she insane? She was like a crazy stalker. This had to stop.

But before she could head back in the direction of the hot ovens, a plastic Wiffle ball hit Harry lightly on the shoulder, and a boy of about eight rushed up. He looked as if he was apologizing, but Harry held on to the ball, a smile on his face. Then he began to demonstrate a pitch, arcing his muscled arm and letting his body follow through.

"Leave," Acey said out loud. "Now."

An elderly man came out the building's front door, weighed down with two bags of trash. Harry handed the ball back to the boy, sprinted over and grabbed a bag. As soon as his back was to the street, Acey skipped out of the doorway and ran back up to Focaccia's. She hopped behind the counter and looked up. Twenty-five after. Whoops.

"You're late," Lydia said, and before Acey could apologize, added, "and I should hope so. How is he?"

Lydia's face was expectant. Acey took off her friend's sunglasses and handed them over.

"I can't believe it myself," Acey said. "But he's… he's…"

Possibly stinking rich. And therefore, not for me.

"You're speechless," Lydia said with a chuckle. "This one must be a real winner."

"Funny you should say that," Acey replied.

Chapter Three

Harry pushed his swivel chair back from his tiny, lopsided desk and wiggled his cramped fingers. He found he could only type for about three hours before he needed to stretch them out. It was pretty pathetic, but it was better than a few months ago, when he began his career as a grant writer. Back then, it only took about sixty minutes before his hands, stiff with the privilege of leisure for most of his life, ached.

Harry's new work carried some irony. He was now writing grant letters to the government for charities and small businesses requesting money that his former self could have just donated if he felt so inclined. But he'd left his inheritance behind, and now his job was to work on behalf of these organizations. He had plenty of fundraising and networking experience from just being a wealthy Wells, but he didn't know, until he began toiling away for a living, that he'd have a knack for doing it full-time.

When he came to New York, he'd brought enough money to give himself a financial cushion while he freelanced. The money was a better reserve than most people had, but was nowhere near the amount of money he was actually entitled to. As he had no résumé to speak of, he'd planned on a period of figuring out what he was capable of. So far, he'd made the right decisions. A rarity for someone accustomed to having accountants and attorneys make his decisions for him.

He checked his watch. One o'clock. Lemonade break. He'd missed his lemonade yesterday when a call to the current charity he was working for ran long. Thank God the call hadn't occurred a day earlier, or Harry might have missed seeing that…that vision on the street outside, and the opportunity to run and help her.

Harry rose and stretched his arms over his head, thinking of Acey Corelli, the wild-haired, fiery-eyed temptress. The way she called him "cowboy," like he was a character actor in an old romantic Western. He wanted to see her again. He hoped his street was her regular route to work, because he'd been glancing out the window every two minutes for the past three days.

He knew her name. He supposed he could look her up…

No, said his relentless conscience. Aside from his vow to build his own life and make his own way in the world, he'd also secretly decided, upon leaving Texas, that he wouldn't get mixed up with any women for the time being. He'd proved to be a danger to himself, and to others. It was too hard to remember the horse, and the pain, and the horror on Lara's face, which had shone so adoringly five minutes earlier when her man and her horse had pranced out into the jumping ring together.

Harry couldn't bear to hurt another woman, and it seemed that was all he knew how to do. He'd made up his mind to just pull himself out of the dating game until he'd convinced himself he'd changed. It had been only six months since arriving here, but Harry had let his old easy habits with women die out.

Harry went to the window and looked out. Dark clouds had been hanging in the sky since late morning. He noted the still-dry sidewalk and decided against his umbrella. But then he saw one other thing on the sidewalk, something that his lemonade could damn well wait for.

It was her. It *was* Acey, walking along his street, weighed down with a plastic bag emblazoned with a supermarket logo. She was carrying it in her arms, and Harry guessed the bag had a hole in it. Lucky for him, because now he could watch her bare, olive-skinned legs as she put one foot in front of the other.

If he hadn't been hypnotized by her swaying walk, Harry wouldn't have noticed her slow down, just a tiny bit, in front of his building. But yes, her pace was definitely waning as she inclined her head toward the brick facade.

Was she admiring Mrs. Stein's purple lilac bushes out front? Harry imagined a woman might be taken with them, but Acey's gaze traveled around the front yard and up the side of the building. Harry took one step back from the window, so he could still see her from the second floor but she hopefully couldn't see him.

Was she possibly looking for him? No. Harry scoffed at his own ego. He had gotten a little too used to beautiful women skulking near his Texas mansion, hoping for a glimpse. Maybe Acey was looking for someone else?

She shrugged, her smooth shoulders lifting the straps of her black tank top up and down. Then she continued on her way, but her bag chose that moment to split open, spilling apples and boxes of raisins all around her.

Without thinking twice about it, Harry hurried outside.

"Acey Corelli," he drawled, "once again cast in the damsel-in-distress role."

"For crying out loud," Acey said. "Do you believe this? I'll have to walk home a different way tomorrow so lightning doesn't strike me right here, too."

Harry squinted up at the blackening sky. "I'd say that's a possibility right now."

"Great. You'd better stand back to avoid being hit."

"I think it would be better if you came in and let me give you a new bag."

"Oh, no, I couldn't put you out again." She seemed more flustered than she ought to.

"You're right," Harry said. "The best thing for you to do, obviously, would be to gather up all your groceries in your arms and just go on home. Here you go. Can you put this mac-n-cheese in your purse? And you can probably fit this in the pocket of your shorts."

Acey laughed. "If you try to slide that banana in my pocket, you'll be seeing me in court, cowboy."

Harry was mortified. "I didn't mean that as a—as a, you know..."

"Hey, I know," Acey said. "I'm just teasing you. You're right. I can't really walk home like this. I'll make it quick."

"Don't," Harry said, but changed it quickly to, "I mean, you don't have to."

He led her up to his apartment for the second time in their brief acquaintance. They had just finished piling groceries on his kitchen table when a clap of thunder crashed, so loud that her hands flew to her ears. Then she checked around the room. "God, I thought that hit us."

He liked the way she said "us."

Then, as if from a giant overturned bucket, rain dumped down, pouring over the windowsills. Harry jumped to close a window and Acey closed the other one while the drops slammed into the glass like BB-gun pellets. Harry said, "I can't let you go out in this. I hope you don't have anywhere you need to be."

"No, it's my day off."

"That doesn't seem too unusual for a Saturday."

"It is where I work." Acey sank to the floor and crossed her legs lotus-style. "Saturday's busy from dawn till dusk. I've been there five years, and I finally got the seniority for Saturdays off."

"Where's this?"

"Focaccia's."

"Oh, up the street? The pizza place? I haven't tried it yet."

"You've been here a few months and you haven't been there yet? What's your problem?"

Harry laughed. Acey was so in-your-face—so open and honest. "I've been eating tons of sandwiches. Heros, that is. I guess I never was much of a pizza person."

"Who's not a pizza person?"

Harry shrugged.

"Come by and order a large pie with everything," Acey continued, "and I guarantee you will become a pizza person after the first bite."

"Does your boss pay you for advertising like this?"

"It's not advertising, it's just the truth. It's the best in New York."

Harry thought that even if Acey had said it was terrible pizza, the worst ever, he would still have planned a trip there. Purely for the service.

The two fell silent for another few minutes. Harry was the sort to enjoy companionable quiet but it seemed his talkative guest might not be, so he said, "Would you like some music?"

Acey brightened. "That would be great." Then she frowned. "Oh, but not if you're going to put on some twangy country stuff. I can't stand it."

Harry walked to the stereo and flipped through his CD collection. "Were you born here, Acey?"

"Born in Queens, then my family moved a whopping ten miles to Valley Stream when I was about four."

"So then, what does a city slicker like you know about country music?"

"Loads."

"Uh-huh." He paused. "Y'all watched *Urban Cowboy* a couple of times and that's it. Am I right?"

Acey looked guilty. "Okay," she admitted. "But how much do I have to hear to know I don't like it?"

"I'll tell you a secret," Harry said, sliding a CD in and pressing Play. "I don't like country music, either." The first chords of a Bruce Springsteen hit filled the room.

Acey grinned. "Now that's more like it, cowboy." She looked down at his boots. "That *is* some secret. I bet you'd have to turn those boots over to the Texas authorities if I ratted you out."

"I trust you."

"Mistake number one." She laughed. "Actually, I'm joking. I'm good with secrets. Got any others you'd like to spill while you're at it?"

Was it his imagination, or did she look as if she really knew something? Could she know him? No, he wasn't nationwide famous. He'd just been locally famous back home. But her teasing tone had an undercurrent of something. "Nope," he told her. "My life—as it is now—is an open book."

"My younger sister writes books."

"Really?" Harry sat down on the floor also, leaning his back against the sofa. "Have I heard of her?"

"No. She hasn't sold one yet. But she's really good. She writes mysteries. It's only a matter of time before everyone knows the name Stephanie Corelli. Then we can move into a bigger place. Or she can just buy me my own." Acey grinned.

"You live together?"

"Yes. Sisters and roomies. She was my only roommate my whole life, actually. I went to community college, and when I was…done, we moved out of our parents' house."

He noticed her hesitation, but didn't comment. "You're very close, then."

"Yeah. It was just the two of us growing up. What about you? Any brothers or sisters?"

"Two younger sisters. They're in Texas, along with everyone else in my family." Harry stopped. He didn't want to get into this topic, get into how his sisters thought he was crazy to leave Texas, how his parents insisted he was not in his right mind, and how he'd yelled back that for the first time in his life, he *was*.

Acey waited. Harry supposed she wasn't used to

conversation with someone like him. Most of the people around here talked like she did, fast and loud and boisterous. It made Harry hyperaware of how he thought out every sentence before he spoke. It wasn't a Southern thing, either—it was a conscious effort to be more deliberate in word and action. He opened his mouth, but was interrupted by another bone-cracking thunderclap.

Acey stuck her fingers in her ears again for a moment, then said, "I hate thunderstorms."

Harry got halfway up, snapped on a lamp next to the sofa and sank back down. "Didn't your parents tell you it was God moving the furniture?" That was the line he remembered from one of his well-meaning nannies.

"They tried to sell me some story like that but I didn't buy it. So Dad got me this book on weather, and I looked it up. I still have to tell myself every time that it's just this big sound of a shock wave made when air is compressed around the lightning. Knowing how it happens makes me feel a little less scared."

"Sounds like your Dad knew what a clever kid he had."

"I think he hoped I would turn out to be something. I did always have big dreams and intentions, but I have a problem with follow-through. That's what Steph says."

"What does Acey say?"

"Acey says, got anything to drink?"

"I know a subject change when I hear it. What's your poison? Soda? Beer?"

"A beer would be excellent."

Harry went into the kitchen, opened two bottles and brought them back into the living room, where Acey was staring out at the rain. Harry handed her a bottle and clinked his with hers. "To skinned knees."

"And Southern hospitality," she said. They both tilted their heads back and drank. "So," Acey said. "Somehow you know about my job, my sister and one dumb hang-up I have. Start talking."

"Oh, is it my turn now?"

Acey made a horrified face.

"I'm kidding, I'm kidding. I like listening to you. You're funny. In a good way," he said, as Acey raised her bottle threateningly.

"At least tell me about your job. Is it freelance?"

"Yes, I've done a few projects now, most of them successful."

"What are you working on today?"

"Right now I'm trying to get a grant for this new cat shelter a few towns away. It's a great place, a no-kill shelter. But when you commit to keeping animals for a long time, you need money to do it."

"Hmm. I admit I thought writing grants sounded boring, but not if you get to help places like that. Have you been to see the shelter?"

"Of course, several times. Every time I go I'm supposed to be there for business but I end up playing with an armful of the cutest cats."

Acey's eyes widened, and she turned her face to the side, muttering something that sounded like, "God, even animals love you." But why would she say that?

"Excuse me?"

"Nothing, nothing. I have a habit of talking to myself all the time."

"You *are* a good conversationalist. I don't blame you for wanting it to go both ways."

"Very funny."

The rain continued to beat down, and small talk kept Harry and Acey busy until their beers were finished.

"Another?" Harry asked, putting out his hand for her bottle.

"No, thanks. I didn't have lunch yet. Any more alcohol and I may say things I'll regret." She stood and stretched her arms out to her sides, then walked toward the kitchen. "I'd better go bag my stuff."

Harry followed her and pulled out two plastic bags from his cabinet. He gave her one, and they bagged her things together.

"Thanks. Hey, you do have photos!" Acey pointed to the refrigerator door. "Who are they?"

"Those are my sisters, Minnie and Corinne."

"Do you miss your family?"

Harry chose his words carefully. "I miss my sisters, mostly. My parents, well…I love them, but distance is the best solution, if you know what I mean."

"I do," Acey said. "My parents finally moved to Florida this year. Though you'd hardly know it by the number of times Ma still calls. She can't miss any quality nagging opportunities."

Harry laughed. "My mother didn't nag me, I'll say that. She was too busy for that."

"Lucky you." And just at that moment, something else on the refrigerator caught Acey's eye. "Hey, you have a lottery ticket."

"Yeah."

"And is it…? Yes, it is, it's from May twenty-fourth. Did you buy it at Bread and Milk? You know that was the winning store, right?"

"It's been the big story every night." Harry couldn't

keep the wryness out of his voice. "Must be a slow news week."

Acey tilted her head. "Don't you think it's exciting? Someone in the neighborhood? A homey?"

"There have to be better things to occupy the public's mind than someone becoming a member of the rich elite."

"Maybe." Acey moved away from the refrigerator but kept her eyes on Harry. "Just think, thirty-five million dollars. All your financial problems solved. Like that." She snapped her fingers.

"More like, his problems are probably just beginning," Harry retorted, failing to keep annoyance out of his voice.

"What are you, crazy? Most people dream of hitting it big."

Harry didn't say, *I'm not most people.*

"I knew a rich guy once," Acey added. "Trust me, he had no problems."

"Did he cause any?" Harry asked.

Acey paused for a long moment. "I still think you should check your numbers," she finally said.

Harry realized the last thing he wanted was to tip this woman off to his sad truth. He reined in his emotion. "The rain's stopped."

"So it has." Acey picked her bags up off the table.

"I'll throw out your apples because they fell in the street. Wait." He reached into a silver bowl on the table and picked out two shiny apples, dropping them into one of her bags. "I bought these yesterday."

"You didn't have to do that."

"I always buy fruits and vegetables and never eat them. I just end up eating take-out food and letting the produce rot. Please take them."

"A'right, thanks. I bet you can tell by my appearance that I *never* waste food." She rolled her eyes.

Harry took her self-deprecating comment as an invitation to sweep his gaze over her body. She was not overweight. She was as lush and ripe as a piece of fruit herself, and when he turned his eyes back to her face, it was the color of the apples in question. She practically ran from the kitchen. Harry followed her but paused to peel the offending lottery ticket out from underneath its magnet. He went to drop it in the trash, but he'd forgotten to replace the bag this morning, so he chucked the ticket on top of the refrigerator. He didn't want to have to see it anymore.

"Thanks," Acey said, edging toward his door. "I mean it. This has been—"

Harry tried to help. "Yeah, it really has been, uh—"

Silence.

"Unexpected," Acey finished, and Harry agreed. *Acey* was unexpected, filling his apartment with exuberance and light, which he was sure he'd miss again the second she left.

He wanted to ask her if she would come by again, or go out somewhere, just spend time with him in some way but his promise to himself was still there, humming through him, stopping him. Acey stood a moment, quiet, and with his untrained eye, he could almost see her own inner struggle. He wondered if it was the same, and he wondered at her reasons. He hoped she'd give in first. If she did, if she asked him out, he could cave. But if she didn't, he knew his resolve was too strong for him to overcome.

She didn't. She put out her hand. "It was so nice meeting you," she said.

He shook it. "Y'all be careful going home now, all right? Walk slow on that knee," he added with a half smile.

"I like that 'y'all' thing," Acey said. Then she blurted, "Oh, I forgot my purse," and she trotted back to the kitchen. When she returned, she looked at him a bit differently, with her head cocked just slightly to one side.

Harry narrowed his eyes with curiosity.

Acey picked up her grocery bags, stepped outside and said over her shoulder, "See ya around, cowboy." Then she clattered down the stairs.

Harry grinned. Everything that woman did was noisy.

"I wasn't stalking him," Acey called, squeezing water out of her hair and into the kitchen sink. A second quick downpour had caught her two blocks from home, drenching her. She wrapped a towel around her head and entered the living room where Steph was sitting, her eyebrows raised in amused fashion.

"I wasn't stalking," Acey repeated.

"Uh-huh," Steph said, leaning back on the sofa and lacing her fingers behind her head.

"I *wasn't*." Acey tucked the towel behind each ear to hear better. "The supermarket run *happened* to take me past his building. And then my bag sort of ripped open, maybe because I sort of absentmindedly picked a hole in the bottom of it with my nail."

"Suddenly this all becomes more believable."

"Listen, I had to meet him again. So my bag breaks, and he comes running like…like…"

"Like what?"

"Like the hero. Every time I see him, he's saving the

day. In the store, he was all sweet to Rosalia, and he said the nicest thing to Cassandra I ever heard, did I tell you?"

"About twenty-three times."

"He helps kids, and elderly people, and me."

"So, is his place papered with hundred-dollar bills?"

"No, it's…totally nothing. It was like, white walls and brown chairs and that's it."

"Doesn't sound very megamillionaire-ish."

"No, I thought the same thing. I talked to him and I felt…" Acey stopped. She'd *felt,* and that was amazing in itself. She'd wrapped up and protected her heart since her bad breakup last year, and she hadn't really enjoyed a conversation with a man in so long.

"Felt what?"

Acey shook her head. "I just figured, it's not him. I mean, he's in this little apartment, doing this freelance grant-writing work for nonprofits that can't be paying him a whole lot, and if he *did* win, he'd probably be making some serious changes. But…" Acey paused for drama.

Steph, who knew her sister's games, waited ten seconds before demanding, "But what?"

"But before I left, I was in his kitchen, and I saw a lottery ticket on the fridge. The date was May twenty-fourth."

Steph jumped a tiny bit. "Did you ask him about it?"

"Yeah, but I tried to be cool."

"Ha!"

"Shut up. I tried to start a conversation about it, but he reacted so strangely. He just about said that winning all that money would *cause* problems, not solve them. He sounded annoyed."

"Did you recognize the numbers? They've been showing them so often on TV…"

"That was another thing. The numbers were folded under. I could read the date but not the numbers."

"Maybe he'd folded it in his pocket when he bought it and stuck it up there like that?"

"Yeah, well, here's the kicker. I forgot my purse, and when I went back to the kitchen to get it, it was gone."

"Your purse was gone?"

"*No*. The ticket. Gone. Disappeared off the refrigerator. So I peeked in the garbage can. The can was empty, not even a trash bag in there. He'd followed me out of the room the first time, so…"

Steph was nodding, her mystery-writing, clue-analyzing mind jumping ahead. "So you think he swiped it out of your sight? Hid it in a safe place?"

"Exactly. Which got me to thinking on my walk home."

"As well it should."

"I thought, for someone so convinced that money causes problems, he still *bought* a ticket. If he's so antimoney, why did he pay a buck to play?"

"Good question."

"Isn't it." Acey plopped herself down on the floor and put her fuzzy-slippered feet on top of her sister's bare ones. "The thing is, he's so…" Her voice trailed off.

"Amazing? Sexy? Wonderful? Gorgeous?"

Acey looked into Steph's face.

"It's okay, hon," Steph said. "I knew you had a thing for him the first time you saw him. You've been going on and on about him even before today's little encounter. Maybe you can ask him out?"

"No. Absolutely not." Acey jerked her head from side to side, and her towel turban collapsed. She threw it to the ground. "What if it turns out he's the one? That he won all that money? And I think that's the case."

"That would be great, right? You wanted it to be a nice person who won. From your description, he's the nicest man who ever walked the streets of New York."

"It would be terrific for him, but I couldn't go out with him. I couldn't have a *relationship* with him."

"Why not?"

Acey was quiet for a minute. "You know why not. I hate talking about it. Even after all this time, I *still* hate thinking about Charlie and what he—" She cut herself off before beginning again. "I'm *never* dating a wealthy man again. I will *never* again be accused of being a gold digger."

"Listen, Charlie's parents had their heads up their behinds when they said that."

"Charlie didn't exactly rush to my defense."

"I think that was less a consequence of his being rich and more a consequence of his being an utter bastard."

"I'm not taking any chances. No rich guys." Acey lay down on the floor. "I liked Harry. Dammit."

"Should we hope he didn't win? That doesn't seem right."

"No."

"Besides," Steph said, "if everything you said is true—that funny business with the ticket, and the weird stuff he said—he *does* sound like the secret winner."

"I know." Acey lay quiet for a moment. "Remember the other night? When we were wondering about why the winner wouldn't come forward and then we thought he might just be scared?"

"Yeah?"

"That could be it. Harry could be scared to have all

that money. Scared it will corrupt him somehow. Cause problems, he said."

"Sounds possible." Steph glanced at her watch. "Time for the news." She hit the power button on the remote and grabbed her notebook. Acey sat watching with her sister through stories on accidents and homicides and world tensions before the lottery took precedence once again.

"Still no word on the winner of the thirty-five-million-dollar lottery jackpot, who bought the lucky ticket at a Valley Stream convenience store," the TV said.

Steph looked at Acey, who took the remote from her and muted the set.

"I can't pursue Harry. I liked him," Acey repeated. "And I'm pretty sure he liked me, at least as a friend. So I can be his friend, and—"

"And what?" Steph asked suspiciously.

"And help him see the light. I can help him—come out of his shell of an apartment and see that having money will be a *good* thing for him, and he can help other people with it, which I'm sure would be important to him."

"You can't let on you know it's him."

"Obviously, no. Then he'd assume I'm out to get my hands on it." She sighed. "God knows, *I'll* never win the lottery, but if I help him accept his destiny, it will feel in some small way like I won, too. You know?"

Steph chewed on her lip. "Yeah," she finally said. "I see what you mean. Especially if he's like you said—a hero, always saving the day."

"Maybe this time," Acey said, "the hero needs someone to save the day for him."

Chapter Four

The door buzzer startled Harry out of slumber. It was just as well, because pressing his right cheekbone against his desk blotter probably wasn't considered an ideal place for a nap. A long nap, he realized, glancing at his clock and seeing it had gone from midafternoon to early evening.

The buzzer blared again and Harry jogged to the living room. "Who is it?" he called. He knew he'd probably have to go outside anyway because the quality of his intercom was terrible, something he had learned when he ended up buying thirteen boxes of Girl Scout cookies his second week here.

What he heard was garbled but sounded an awful lot like, "Pizza delivery!"

"Uh, I think you have the wrong apartment," Harry replied, and listened.

"Pizza," he heard again.

"But I didn't order a pizza."

"That's the problem, sir."

Huh? Wait…

Harry went down to the front door and there was Acey, holding out a huge flat box.

"Howdy," he said with a grin.

"Hey, there. Thought I'd kill two birds with one stone—repay your niceness yesterday *and* prove to you how right I am about Focaccia's." She handed him the box. "There you go."

Harry patted his pockets. "Sorry, I'm wiped out. I can't tip you."

"What a cheapskate," she said, laughing.

"How about I offer you a slice? If you don't have dinner plans, of course."

"As it happens, I don't."

"Unless you're tired of pizza."

"I never get tired of pizza," Acey said, following him into his apartment. Harry lifted the lid on the box and took a big sniff.

"Everyone does that," Acey said.

"It smells amazing."

"I didn't top it. I didn't know if you were a vegetarian or had an aversion to anything. It's best plain, anyway. Then you can taste it. Are you really sure you don't mind my dropping in like this?"

"Of course not." Harry put the box on the table and took two plates from the cabinet. "It's real nice."

"I'm glad. I was thinking it had been so long since I met a real friend."

Harry's hand stilled on a glass for a fraction of a second, then he carried on setting the table. There was no mistaking Acey's emphasis on the word "friend." *It's just as well,* he thought. *I don't want any entanglements. And she's real outgoing and probably has lots of male friends. And maybe a boyfriend.* Though wouldn't she be bringing pizza home to her boyfriend after work?

Well, if she was coming here and throwing the word *friend* around, Harry thought, then his problems were pretty much solved, weren't they?

He turned. Acey sat at the table and smiled. She was wearing a low-cut white clingy shirt, and a tiny sliver of a pale pink bra strap peeked through. A strand of little pink plastic-looking beads dipped into her deep cleavage.

Harry was suddenly grateful for his impromptu nap. He had a sinking feeling another sleepless night was ahead.

"Care to eat alfresco?" he asked.

"Sure."

"I have a little porch off the—" damn "—off the bedroom."

Acey seemed unfazed. "Lead the way."

"Grab the box."

Hoping he'd left nothing offensive in plain sight, he led Acey through the apartment and out onto his tiny porch, where he had a table and two little folding chairs. Luckily, they had dried out in the sun today after yesterday's downpour. He gestured to one. Acey sat and dished out two slices.

"I only have regular soda, not diet," Harry said. "I hope that's all right."

"Do I look like I drink diet soda?" Acey asked. Harry wished she wouldn't keep calling attention to her appearance, because it made it hard for him to try to ignore it. "Eat," she commanded.

Harry took a bite, then another, then another, and was halfway through his slice before he remembered to look up. "Wow."

"Did I lie?"

"No. It tastes… The sauce is almost sweet. It goes beyond expectations."

Acey nodded.

"And now I'm very angry at you," Harry added.

"Why?"

"Because now that I know how good this pizza is, I'll have to buy new jeans when I gain forty pounds."

Acey chewed and looked down at the street. "I've never paid full price for a stitch of clothing in my life. Let me know when you need those jeans and I'll give you some tips."

"Deal."

"Although," she said, taking another enormous bite and shielding her full mouth with one hand, "I must say it would be nice to afford some really fancy designer clothes. Just once. Don't you think?"

Harry felt a twinge. Acey struck him as a very hard worker. Yesterday, she'd mentioned working weekends for years. She probably deserved to have any beautiful thing she wanted. Harry used to throw clothes, jewelry, expensive trinkets at women who barely looked at them, women whom he was merely passing time with. "But that outfit you have on now looks real nice," he said.

Acey blushed a flattering pink. To match that insistent strap. "Well," she said, "you probably wouldn't be into that anyway. Clothes are mostly a girl thing."

"Certainly."

She fell silent then and Harry thought it odd. She seemed not to be relaxing within the conversation but rather to be searching for words, and after knowing her only a short time, Harry would have guessed she rarely ran out of words. Or questions.

He reminded himself he wasn't on a date with Acey, but he wasn't ever the kind of man who had circles of female friends, so he would have to rely on date techniques, at least in this get-to-know-you phase of talk. "What do you like to do?" he finally tried. "When you're not working, that is."

Acey swallowed, then she sighed. It was a great sigh. She used her whole head to do it—first sucking in a lungful of air through her open mouth, holding it for a hot second, then arching her neck and blowing the air through puffed lips up toward the sky. Then she rolled her eyes, like an ending punctuation.

Harry nodded with appreciation and clapped his hands four times. "Very nice. The Oscar for most dramatic moment goes to…Acey Corelli." Acey curtsied with the top half of her body. "Now," Harry added, "how about telling me why I deserved *that?*"

"Oh," Acey said. "I'm sorry. It's just that that question is always the first thing every guy asks me on a blind date."

Oops. "I am interested," Harry said quickly. "It wasn't just idle shrimp-cocktail chatter."

"You actually spring for appetizers on first dates? Very impressive. Grant writing must treat you well."

Harry winced inwardly.

"Anyway, the sigh was not because you asked but because I never have a good answer."

"Let me be the judge."

Acey considered, and into Harry's mind floated answers he'd heard over candlelit dinner dates past. *What do I like to do?* a collective breathless female voice said in his memory. *I like to ski in Aspen...*

"I like to play handball with Steph in the schoolyard..."

...I like to party all night at the hottest clubs...

"...I like to sleep as late as possible and leave my pajamas on until it's time to go to bed again..."

...I like to jet off to Monte Carlo or Paris for the weekend...

"...I used to like to have Sunday dinner at Ma's once in a while, but I'd never admit that to her..."

...What do you like? I bet I'd like it, too, baby...

"...and I like to read and watch videos and just hang out. I'm boring as hell, when it comes right down to it."

"I don't agree," Harry said. "In fact, those are the most intriguing and unique answers I've ever heard."

"You must know a real bunch of airheads, then."

"You have no idea." Harry took a long sip of soda. "Why do you think you're boring? Is it that you'd rather be doing other things?"

Acey regarded him with respect. "That's pretty insightful. You're saying if I was interested in my own life, then I would just expect it to interest you, too." She paused. "I don't dislike my life or what I do. It would just be nice to...enhance it once in a while. See places I've never been, and do things there I've never experienced."

"Ski in Aspen? Shop in Paris? Play baccarat in Monte Carlo?" Harry couldn't help himself.

"Not all the time. I would want beautiful exotic places to stay beautiful and exotic. But to know I could do that, once in a while, would be, well, it would just be nice," she said. "Don't you think?"

Guilt came in a wave over Harry, but it was replaced by something else. While he was trying to figure it out, Acey said, "I don't know about the skiing, though. I mean, you witnessed the other day how difficult it is for me to just walk down a street without falling on my butt."

Harry smiled, but distractedly. In his head, he was close to something. Acey didn't notice his sudden lack of honest good humor. She just took another bite and refilled her glass, misjudging the foam level rising on top. She leaned over to suck the foam noisily before it spilled over. Then she eyed him. "That was pretty good. Don't you think?"

Don't you think? Don't you think? That was it. She asked him for his opinion often. And usually it was over...money. *It would be nice to have money, don't you think? To afford clothes, to see new places, don't you think?*

Harry *thought,* all right. He thought just maybe, this woman knew a little more about him than she was letting on. But how could she? He'd never laid eyes on her before the other day, and he was *certain* he'd have remembered her. But as soon as he did meet her, she popped up all the time. In the store, on his street, in his apartment, stretching cheese in a long string from her lips.

He had talked more with this woman than he had with any member of his family in the past six months. His family... Harry dropped a glob of sauce on his pant leg and mopped it up with a stray napkin. When he last talked to Minnie, she'd told him the rest of the family worried about his long absence, and wondered when he'd be back to claim his rightful place as the heir of the Wells ranching estate. He knew he was frustrating them, especially his father.

How far would his father go to find out Harry's every move? Was Acey Corelli really Miss Corelli, Ace Detective?

"I'm totally pigging out here," Acey said, taking another slice.

If this was a routine, it was brilliant. Some outstanding cover.

"That's okay," Harry said, keeping up his end of talk so Acey wouldn't suspect he was possibly on to her game. "I was thinking, maybe I'd come see you at Focaccia's one of these days. Maybe tomorrow?"

"You can't get enough, eh? I mean of the pizza, not me," she added.

His question didn't rattle her in the slightest. She was either a really cool player or she really did work in the pizza place and did the private investigating work on the side, Harry thought. Maybe freelance.

He recalled her rapid-fire interview-type questions in the street yesterday. He'd thought it was charming at the time. Was it, in fact, her job?

The next half hour's dialogue would have sounded to any casual observer as normal chat between new friends. But Harry was distracted by every word, analyzing each of her sentences in his mind, turning them over to examine her motives for everything she said. It was not unlike when he'd seen that psychologist after his accident. Back then, Harry had answered questions by meting each of his thoughts out with measured care, trying to hear himself as the doctor would and then trying to stay one step ahead of her. By the second session, the psychologist had sussed him out. "This would be much easier," she'd suggested patiently, "if you'd just be honest with me and let me help you instead of worrying about my opinion of you." This masterful revelation had almost convinced Harry to not return for a third session.

Now, he found himself again attempting to stay one step ahead, but it was especially hard with a fast talker like Acey. Finally, Harry was too stressed to continue. He wanted to straighten out this suspicion before he liked her so much that he inadvertently trusted her with any real information about himself. He made up an excuse about being tired, and Acey took the immediate hint, helped him clean up and invited him to stop by her workplace anytime.

"This was really fun," she said.

Harry beat her to her inevitable next line. "Don't you think?"

She winked. Harry watched her shapely body sway out the door and hated himself. He wasn't sure if it was because he wouldn't allow himself to be taken with her, or because he couldn't.

"Wayne, it's me."

"Me? Sorry, the only Me I know was the Me who promised to call two weeks ago and never did. This can't be that Me."

Harry grimaced. He hadn't been able to get any work done after Acey sashayed out his door two hours ago. When he'd finally picked up the phone to call his brother-in-law, the current torment had been fully expected. "Very funny."

"Wait a darn minute. The voice sounds familiar," Wayne drawled. "Like this guy I used to hang out with. But one day he took off. He gave me some reasons like starting over, bettering himself, but personally, I think it was because he was through with the available women here in Texas and needed to meet a fresh crop in a different state. I hear they're beautiful in New York."

"I sure do appreciate the way you make things real easy for me, Wayne. It makes me *want* to pick up the phone and call you when I promise I will."

"Ah, Harry, I'm just messing with your scrawny head."

"Yeah, yeah," Harry said. Wayne was Minnie's husband before he became Harry's best friend, but that didn't stop either of them in the past three years from making up for delayed childhood-pals time. Rather than feeling threatened by her brother's close relationship with Wayne, Minnie was delighted the men had taken to each other. Harry knew she had worried, when she first brought Wayne home from college, that her parents might take issue with his being a car mechanic instead of a trust-fund baby like herself. By the end of Wayne's first family dinner, however, he had charmed Harry's mother with his easy jokes and good looks, and Harry's father never again had any other mechanic so much as glance in the direction of his Bentley.

Wayne and Minnie were the only ones who knew Harry was in New York. Harry had had to tell someone, in the event of an emergency, and it stood to reason he would trust his best buddy. Of course, as Harry and every other man on earth knew, when you trust any male buddy, you also must, by extension, trust his wife. Minnie's reliability was slightly more rubbery, capable of bending under the will of her parents and older sister, but Harry was counting on her not wanting to disappoint Wayne by blabbing.

"Did you call me just to see how I'm getting along?" Wayne teased. "Just to hear my voice?"

"Not quite," Harry answered, rolling his eyes.

"I saw that," Wayne said immediately, and Harry laughed. "Whatever it is," Wayne continued, "I'm glad you finally did call. We miss you, buddy. Did I ever tell you that when you first left, Minnie sat me down, all serious, and then gave me a little speech all about how just because my friend moved away, doesn't mean we still can't stay in touch? It was hilarious, like she was talking to a six-year-old."

"Was she busting your balls or is it possible she was practicing how to talk to a kid?"

"Why would she do that?"

Wayne didn't quite get it sometimes, but Harry was happy to hammer it home in this case. "Don't be a bonehead. I'm sure you know she thinks it's high time you two, ah, became more than two."

"You mean…"

"Reproduce."

"Really?" Wayne sounded terrified. "Now?"

"I'm pretty sure not right this second, but I have a feeling this is something you are going to want to work out with her. In the meantime, I have a problem."

"What is it?" He had Wayne's full attention again. "Is everything all right?"

"Sure. Or…I don't know. I met a woman."

"Great!" Wayne waited a beat, and added, "Or, not great?"

"Not a woman I want to date. I'm not doing that these days. As you are aware."

"Painfully."

"I'm busy with other things."

"This *is* Harry, isn't it? I haven't been talking for the last five minutes to a wrong number, have I?"

"The thing is," Harry said, ignoring the jab, "this woman is acting strange. She's saying some weird things to me, and it got me wondering…y'all don't know if my father was considering, ah, hiring a private investigator, do you? To keep tabs on me?"

Wayne paused. "You think this woman is a P.I.?"

"You don't understand. It's the way she talks, the kind of questions she asks me. She's not like other women. She says she wants to be my friend."

Wayne chuckled. "Sounds like *that's* the part that's tough for you to swallow."

"Believe me, that's not it." Well, maybe a little bit it. Harry shook it off. "And she's suddenly around all the time. I mean, *all* the time."

"So tell her to bug off."

"I can't do that."

"You can't do that? Or you don't want to do that?"

Harry answered with silence, giving Wayne the freedom to interpret as he saw fit. "Have you heard anything?"

"Well," Wayne began, and stopped. Harry held his breath. "About a week ago, I'da thought you crazy to ask," Wayne continued. "But just the other day, I happened to overhear a conversation between your parents when we were over there. It was before dinner, and I was watchin' the game with the sound off and I heard your name and I…kinda eavesdropped."

"Attaboy."

"They were arguing about you. Your father is still

real unhappy about not knowing your whereabouts. Your mother's not worried. She says you can take care of yourself. She's just disappointed at you turnin' your back on them. That's what she said."

Harry felt a stab of guilt in his gut, but reminded himself that his actions were for everyone's long-term good. "I feel bad for staying underground, but…"

"You don't need to explain your reasons to me," Wayne said. "Anyway, your father had worked himself up into a lather, and it sounded to me like it was because the whole thing is out of his control."

"That's likely."

"Then I heard him tell your mother that he was going to hire a private investigator to find you."

Aha. He sure did know his father. "That would be easy cash for the lucky P.I. I didn't exactly change my identity. I wasn't trying to drop off the earth. Just get away for a while."

"Well, hold on," Wayne said. "Your mother was horrified. She said that not only was it a completely undignified and classless thing to do, it would backfire in his face if you found out about it."

"Damn right."

"She made your father promise not to do it. And, he did."

Harry raised his brows. "Are you sure?"

"I heard him myself. 'You have my word,' he said. And your mother capped it off by saying that if the topic ever even came up again, he'd be sorry."

A wave of relief washed over Harry. His father had his faults: control issues, business obsessions, coldness. But one thing his father didn't do was go back on his word. "A man is only as good as his word," he said very often, and not just to his children when caught in minor fibs. Harry had heard him issue that stern advice time and again to several young upstarts in his employ.

So that was it. Acey Corelli was just Acey Corelli.

"So," Wayne said. "Problem solved. Which leaves you with another problem, that Miss New York is just sweet on you. Though I wouldn't consider that a problem."

Harry sighed.

"Want some advice?"

"No," Harry said quickly.

"Tough. Here it is. You went pretty far away for an opportunity to start over. So don't be looking the other way if the right opportunity comes knocking. Hear me?"

"Yeah, I hear you."

"So, do all the guys there walk around saying 'fuggedaboutit' like in the movies?"

Harry laughed. "Yeah, they do. And the food here is like nothing else."

"Sounds like my kind of place."

The men said their goodbyes and hung up. Harry lay back on his sofa and contemplated one long ceiling crack that ran like a raging river over his head and halfway across the room.

Acey wasn't a private investigator. But even armed with this new information, her behavior still seemed a bit off to Harry. There was always an outside chance she just knew who he was. She might be a business-page reader, and was familiar with his father's ranching empire. Although he couldn't imagine why a restaurant worker would be interested in the ranching business in the first place, much less remember the Wells name days later. Maybe she read something about his accident a year ago?

And there was the issue of her mentioning money, several times too many. She didn't seem like a money-grubber, though, or maybe Harry just didn't want to think she was like other women. She was more of a dreamer.

Even though he'd only eaten a couple of hours ago, Harry was feeling a bit of an appetite again. A little trip to Focaccia's tomorrow afternoon wouldn't be completely out of the question. His eyelids drooped, and the ceiling river ran blurry for a few moments before Harry fell asleep.

Staggering under the weight on one shoulder, Acey hefted five boxes onto the counter and bellowed, "Five large, all anchovy!"

She heard a couple of people mutter "blecch" and, secretly, she had to agree. That was a monumental amount of anchovy, even for a devoted fan, which she most definitely was not. A man three people back from the counter put up his hand and called, "Anchovy pizzas!" Awed customers parted to clear his path, and Acey took his money, careful not to lean too close to his face. One couldn't be certain of the freshness of the breath of a guy who pounded anchovy like that.

Anthony had the afternoon off, and Acey was grateful for the relative calm that came with separating the lovebirds for a shift.

Steve was working instead. He was a quiet young guy just out of college who'd been working in Focaccia's for the past two months while he searched for a professional job. Steve was as thin as a twig, chiefly because as a vegan, twigs were the only things he was allowed to consume. One day, Acey'd asked him about his culinary decisions. It turned out, not to her surprise, that Steve's girlfriend of one year was a vegan and, under her ceaseless pressure, he'd chosen love over food. More than once since their chat, though, Acey had seen his gaze linger with love at a large pepperoni pie. Acey worried for him—Focaccia's could well bring that relationship to its knees. She hoped that if they did break up, Steve would find himself a nice girl who loved to cook and who would put some literal meat on those skinny bones of his.

The lunch rush was still daunting but was beginning its daily dwindle, and as Acey handed someone change and a bag of garlic knots, she heard Lydia hiss in her ear, "Oooh, baby, I could go for a slice of what just walked in."

Acey's first instinct was to look skyward rather than at the door. Lydia had a crush on half the guys who wandered into Focaccia's. Acey knew Lydia was faithful to Anthony—even on the days she threatened not to be—but she remained an ardent window shopper. If Acey allowed herself to be distracted every time Lydia swooned over a customer, a massive hunger revolt would very likely ensue.

"Thanks and see you soon," Acey said to a retreating couple.

Lydia, not to be ignored today, got close to Acey again. "And listen to that sweet thing come clonking in here in those boots. Haven't seen anything like him in a while."

Then Lydia started humming. It took Acey a moment to discern the tune, what with Lydia's nasal intonation and the perennial easy-listening soundtrack in the background, but it sounded like...the theme to *Bonanza*?

Acey dropped her order pad on the floor, not accidentally, and scooted over to the end of the counter. She peered around it, and saw a half-dozen pairs of customer feet. One pair of flip-flops. Ew, someone needed a serious pedicure. Three sets of scuffed sneakers. One painfully high pair of stiletto sandals.

And one pair of cowboy boots, male, poking out from worn blue denim.

Harry.

A little jolt of energy shot from her own feet to the ends of her hair. The rare occasions when Acey's plans turned out right made her ecstatic. She'd really turned on the charm yesterday to sell herself as someone who'd make a fun, earnest pal. Too bad she couldn't add "honest" to that list. She brushed the thought away. Her knowledge of his winning ticket—and by now, she and Steph had convinced themselves the winner just *had* to be Harry—was the only thing she intended to lie about, and anyway it wasn't really an outright lie. Just something she wouldn't mention. Even when he collected, and Acey would make sure he would, Acey would keep her prior deduction to herself. It wouldn't serve any purpose to tell him.

Acey realized that although she had hoped Harry would come to see her here at work, she hadn't planned further than that. She had no idea what to say or what to suggest they do. She decided to follow his lead. If he contributed equally to their friendship, he would never suspect that Acey had blueprinted the whole thing to begin with.

"Acey, are you okay?"

Steve's gentle voice startled her and she scrambled to an upright position. "Yes. Why?"

Steve looked down at the floor and back at Acey. "Uh, no reason. Can you help out?"

"Of course. I'm sorry."

"I'm sorry, too. It's just that Lydia's abandoned me and the phone's ringing."

"What the heck is she doing?" Acey grabbed the phone and whirled to face the counter as she answered, "Focaccia's!" Then her eyes widened.

Lydia was chattering nonstop to Harry while Steve took care of the only other customer left. Acey couldn't listen to Lydia and the phone order at the same time, so she forced herself to write on her pad.

Lydia's voice cut through Acey's concentration. "I have a great pair of red cowboy boots myself. My boyfr— I mean, my *brother* bought them for me. He's the best."

Lydia was one of five children. All female.

"So that was a small with peppers and mushrooms?" Acey asked.

"No," the pissed-off caller said. "Peppers and olives."

"Right, sorry."

Lydia cracked her gum loud enough to be heard fifteen feet away. Harry winced.

"Did you get that?" the caller asked.

"Get what?" Acey asked back.

"A two-liter of root beer, I *said!*"

Acey surveyed her pad. She'd written that down already. "I got that. Is that it?"

Lydia had taken her ponytail down. She flipped her blond hair over her right shoulder, and after the swish fell, Acey could see Harry's face again. This time he saw Acey, too. He smiled at her.

The phone clicked loudly in her ear. She had no idea if the customer had added anything to his order or had hung up in frustration and would never come in. She handed the pad to Steve, then sauntered over to Lydia, who was saying, "Of course, I can usually catch *The Beverly Hillbillies* on TV late at night, but you have to admit that show's more fun if you're a little bit drunk—"

"Hey, Harry," Acey said.

"Hi, Acey."

Lydia stopped midword, as if the needle had been abruptly lifted off her record.

"I needed a break," Harry continued, "and thought I could convince you to take one, too. That is, if your coworkers don't mind." He beamed at Lydia, who missed it because she was staring at Acey.

"This is... You know this... You...?" Lydia tried.

Acey rescued her. "Harry, this is Lydia Mancini. Her dad owns this joint. Lydia, this is Harry, a new friend of mine."

"Nice to meet you, Lydia."

Lydia responded by whimpering.

"Do you mind if I sit with Harry for five minutes?" Acey asked her. "Seeing as it's cleared out in here."

Lydia nodded absently. "I have to call Anthony," she said.

"Is Anthony your brother?" Harry asked.

"Uh, no." Lydia began to drag herself away, then stopped. She turned to Acey. "Hey, uh, that doctor's appointment the other day...?"

"Yeah," Acey affirmed.

"Oh," Lydia said, perking up. "*Oh.* Great. Take your time." She rushed off.

"Doctor's appointment?" Harry asked as Acey led him to a booth and sat across from him. "Everything all right?"

"Everything's turned out great. Very good news. I love getting good news. Don't you?"

Harry narrowed his eyes. Just a fraction, and it lasted for such a split second, Acey wasn't entirely sure she even saw it. How could she have seen it? It would have been the expression of a man who knew she wasn't acting like herself, and there was no way Harry could know she wasn't acting like herself because he had practically just met her. Although, Acey had to admit silently, it was getting difficult to act at all. Her real self wouldn't constantly go on about wishing she had money and trying to pry the truth out of someone with leading questions. He wasn't biting anyway. It appeared she was going to have to change her tack.

To what?

Follow his lead, Acey reminded herself.

"They work y'all pretty hard here, huh?" Harry asked. "This place must do great business."

"Oh, yeah."

"Speaking of business, I was just watching a business report on CNN before I came here." And Harry launched into a two-minute recap of the day's business news. Stocks, mutual funds, some other stuff. It wasn't that Acey couldn't comprehend it. She had taken some business courses at community college and done well enough. No, what perplexed Acey was why exactly Harry was yapping on about the world of finance. It wasn't exactly friendly chitchat.

Harry stopped, and Acey realized he was waiting for a response. "I'm sorry, I don't follow the stock market so I'm afraid I—" She cut herself off. Maybe Harry was so enthusiastic to talk business news because in the back of his head, he knew it was about to become important in his life. If Acey had had thirty-five million dollars dropped into her lap, she'd make sure she was up-to-date with stock market activity, too.

"No, I'm sorry," Harry countered, appearing surprised at her answer. "I've watched those reports all my life. It's always been of…some interest to me. I brought it up because you seemed like the kind of woman who might be interested in it, too."

"Really?" Acey had a hard time believing that.

"Well, you've said more than once that you dream of having money and I thought possibly you'd be checking out how the people who *do* have money spend it."

Acey didn't like the direction of this conversation. She needed to turn it around. "Whoa. I seem to recall someone saying the first time I met him that money was practically the root of all evil. So how come it interests you enough to watch news about it?"

"It's precisely because I'm aware of its place in the world that I feel the way I do."

Yikes. Okay, then. Acey still had her job cut out for her. Apparently, his feelings on the topic ran deeper than she'd originally anticipated. So how to set about changing his stubborn mind?

"So you never watch business news?" Harry asked.

Speaking of stubborn. "No. And even if I did, I never retain anything. I have this terrible memory. I'd like to say it's because I'm getting old, but I've always been like that. I guess I'm still getting old, though."

Harry chuckled. "How old are you?"

"Twenty-seven."

Harry shook his head sympathetically. "Wow. You are getting up there. I hope you have a good nursing home picked out. You don't want to wait until the last minute with that."

"In that case, you must have had one picked out for some time now. Any suggestions?"

"Touché." Harry laughed. "I've only got three years on you, in case you were wondering."

"I wasn't."

They grinned at each other, and Acey felt a pang in her chest. She didn't venture to guess why. She ignored it and forged ahead. "So, what brings you to this lovely establishment today, by the way?"

"Just the chance of a chat with my charming new friend."

Another pang. "You met your goal, then."

"I did. And maybe a slice of pizza for the road?"

"Sure thing." Acey stood and went behind the counter, trying not to notice Lydia's beyond-curious-and-into-nosy expression. She cut Harry a generous slice and he paid her, touching her fingers with his as she took the five-dollar bill.

Acey had taken money from probably every person in Valley Stream, so it stood to reason that she'd probably touched more hands than a mayoral candidate. She never noticed smoothness, warmth, softness—until now. *Now* she was aware. Her senses stretched the small second of contact into something she expected would linger in her memory.

She pulled away and popped the register. The *ding!* spooked her for the first time ever, and she jumped slightly. She picked up Harry's change with her fingernails and dropped it without contact into his open palm.

"Nice nails," Harry said, and Acey had a feeling it was to let her know he'd noticed her deliberate action.

"Thanks."

"You want to hang out on your next day off?"

Acey cleared her throat. "That's tomorrow. I have split weekends."

"Great. Let's meet somewhere."

"Um." She was having trouble thinking. And talking. And, like, breathing. "How about in front of the travel agency right near Bread and Milk? It's about equidistant from where we both live. Then we can think of something to do." In fact, as she spoke, a brilliant brain wave was happening to her. An idea that could help Harry.

"Noon?"

"You underestimate how late I like to sleep on my days off. Make it one."

Just then, Anthony swung into the restaurant, and bellowed, "Lydia!"

"I'm right here," Lydia told him. "What's with all the screaming?"

"Guess who just got you Madonna tickets?"

Lydia shrieked. "What? Anthony!"

"Fourth row, baby!"

Lydia squealed again and leaped over the counter. "How did you swing that? Did you win the freaking lottery or something?"

Acey glanced at Harry to check his reaction to that little outburst. His eyes were wide. *Ha-ha, caught you,* Acey thought. But his eyes stayed wide. She followed his gaze to where Lydia and Anthony were kissing, with copious tongue usage.

Then she looked back at Harry, whose wide-eyed look was replaced with an admiring, "Attaboy!" expression.

Men. Acey sighed.

Chapter Five

Anyone who'd ever made a date with Acey Corelli inevitably ended up waiting for her. Acey ran late every day, it was true, but it was usually for an endearing reason, like she was ransacking her closet for the perfect outfit, or she spontaneously decided to pick up flowers for a friend. Whatever the occasion, Acey had never before found herself in the position she was in now: twenty minutes early.

Like a restless panther, she paced in front of Go-Around Travel. She checked her watch every two minutes, but she couldn't make time move any faster. Finally, she just resigned herself to staring into the display window, trying to prepare her game plan. She had run the idea by Steph last night.

"Acey," she'd said, "here's what I've learned from

every writing instructor I've ever had. 'Show, don't tell.' Anything you can concretely *show* Harry the New Millionaire will make a much bigger impact than anything you could *say* to him. Show him something that will make him see money will do him good, not harm."

The travel agency, both women had decided, was an excellent place for showing.

The window was filled with big plastic flowers and pictures of beaches and impossibly huge cruise ships. Acey didn't know what Harry would be into, but she intended to find out. She felt a little tingle of pleasure, her body nearly tricking her into believing it was due to the prospect of finding out Harry's preferences.

Her brain reminded her body that the pleasure was in the altruistic task, not in its unwitting recipient. Her body retaliated by forcing her brain to conjure up a picture of Harry's smile. Then her brain transformed it into an image of Charlie's sneer. Her body recoiled in horror.

"Take that," Acey muttered.

"Take what?" she heard behind her and whirled around.

Harry was chuckling. Giggling, almost.

"Let me give ya a tip, cowboy," Acey said through gritted teeth as soon as she caught her breath. "I don't know what it's like down in Texas, but when you sneak up on someone in New York, you put your life in serious danger." She put her hand on her thumping heart, which she assumed was from fright and not the way the short sleeves of Harry's blue T-shirt strained and failed to contain his biceps.

Harry backed away a few steps, putting his hands in front of his face. "Please, don't hurt me. Any thoughts on what you'd like to do today?"

"Not really," Acey said. "But while we're here, I need to run in and grab something for Steph."

"Is she going on vacation?" Harry asked, opening the door and holding it for Acey.

"Hardly. Her latest manuscript has some scene that takes place in Greece and she wanted me to pick up some brochures for research," Acey replied, grateful to Steph for manufacturing the excuse last night.

The door closed behind them and Acey shivered in her green tank top. Go-Around Travel was air-conditioned to arctic temperatures. Acey wondered if this was deliberately subliminal, to give customers that little added motivation to travel to a warm destination. Come to think of it, maybe subliminal was the way to go for her, too. If Acey could find some way to knock Harry unconscious, like accidentally hit him with the door on the way out, or... No, that would be kind of mean. Maybe if she sneaked into his apartment while he slept, and whispered in his ear, "Thirty-five million, thirty-five million," then he would sleepwalk over to the lottery headquarters to collect his prize.

Of course, now she was thinking of what Harry would look like sleeping, and how close she would be to his lips if she were whispering in his ear. Not cool.

There were two middle-aged women behind large cluttered desks, and both were assisting clients. One of them called over to Acey and Harry, "If you have a seat, one of us will be with you very soon."

"We don't need to book anything right now," Acey said. "We'd just like to grab some brochures on Greece."

The woman nodded and pointed to the wall behind Harry. He turned and scanned down a few plastic racks until he found three glossy brochures. He flipped one open for Acey. The blue water of the Aegean Sea sparkled out from the pages, beckoning. "It looks beautiful, doesn't it?" Acey said. "I'd go here."

She waited for some response. He just flipped through the pages, his face giving nothing away. Maybe Greece didn't interest him.

"Where would you like to go?" Acey asked him.

"With you?"

Acey felt herself blush, which was aggravating. "No. With yourself. Where would you go? Pick somewhere you've never been. That you're dying to see. If time and…money…were no object at all."

Harry stared into space for a few moments longer than she'd thought he would. If she asked anyone else that question, they would pop right out with someplace they'd like to see. Everyone had a dream, as far as she knew.

"I'm not sure."

"Oh, come on. You've got the whole world at your feet. You know, theoretically," she added.

The agent who had pointed to the brochures ushered a happy couple out the door and turned to Acey and Harry. "Are you two sure you don't need any help?"

"Yes, we're just trying to get ideas," Acey said.

"Well," the agent said enthusiastically, "the couple that just left are going to Rio de Janeiro. It's gorgeous there."

"It is," Harry agreed, and Acey cocked an eyebrow at him. "From what I've heard," he added.

"I know, let's ask an expert," Acey told him. Then she addressed the agent. "If you could go anywhere in the world, money being no object—"

"I envy you if that's the position you're in," the agent cut in with a laugh.

"Believe me, *I'm* not," Acey said, glancing at Harry. He didn't seem to notice. "But if you were," Acey continued to the woman, "where would you go?"

The agent thought for a moment. "I think I'd pick a safari. It's the trip of a lifetime. A few of our clients went to Kenya and said it's an experience like no other."

"You've never done *that,* I bet," Acey said to Harry.

"No, I haven't."

"Can we get some safari information, too?" Acey asked the agent.

The agent practically ran to the back of the office and Acey felt a little bit bad for leading her on. She imagined the woman would get a huge commission for booking that kind of jaunt. The agent returned with an armful of magazines. "Will you be coming back here soon?" she asked hopefully, handing Acey the literature.

"I promise you, if a safari is in our future, we won't book it anywhere else," Harry drawled, and the agent beamed.

Once again, Acey thought, *Mr. Personality. Putting everyone at ease.* Thinking this kept her from actively thinking the other thing that popped into her head: the way Harry said "our future."

"Ready?" he asked Acey, and she nodded, feeling flushed despite the tundra temperature. She shook her head when Harry then asked if she wanted him to carry the catalogs. She realized she needed something to clutch to her chest. Her breasts were a little, uh, pointy. Purely due to the air-conditioning, she admonished herself.

Harry held the door open for her. The agent called an overly cheery "Bye now!" and Acey wondered if she was gaping at Harry's butt as he walked out.

"Guess we're going to have to avoid catching her eye

whenever we walk past this place, at least for the near future," Harry said as they turned right at the corner and strolled down Sunrise Highway. Cars whizzed past, kicking up a breeze. It blew Acey's unruly hair around her head and into her mouth, where it stuck to her pink lip gloss.

She spat out some strands. "Maybe a safari is perfect for you. Just think. Riding along in a Jeep in Kenya, taking fantastic photographs of lions and elephants. And zebras and gazelles and—"

"Sounds like a trip you'd love. Why don't you go?"

"No way." Acey shook her head regretfully. "It's thousands of dollars. In my whole life, I could never afford that."

"What makes you think *I* could?"

Whoopsy—obviously her words had pushed him a *bit* too much. "I'm just assuming you're fantastic at your job," Acey replied, silently congratulating herself on a good save. "Come on. I've seen your way with people. You can sell raspberry Sno-Kones to a penguin. Grant writing must be pretty lucrative for you. You can, ah, save money in no time. 'The trip of a lifetime,' that woman in the travel place said. Don't you think?"

Harry looked skeptical.

"I'm just a girl who can barely pay her phone bill," Acey continued. "Plus, khaki really isn't my color."

"Hmm."

Harry didn't say anything more, and Acey felt control of the situation slipping through her well-manicured fingers. He was supposed to say, *Hey, a safari is a great idea. You know, the world really is my oyster. I haven't told anyone this, but I won the lottery.*

And thanks to you, I can get started on my luxurious new life...

"Remember when you asked me if I ride in rodeos?" Harry asked.

Acey blinked at the abrupt subject change and spit more hair off her sticky lips. "Uh, yeah. But you said you didn't."

"Is that the kind of thing you're interested in?"

"What?"

"Horses?" He paused. "Ranching?"

A horn blasted in the street, followed by a woman's voice shrieking four-letter words. Acey looked over at the street and saw a fat man crossing the three-lane street illegally, flashing a fleshy middle finger at the irate driver. "Sure. I'm totally into ranching," Acey said. "As you can see, Valley Stream is the perfect place for that kind of hobby."

They turned right onto Rockaway Avenue.

"It was a silly question," Harry conceded. "I was just wondering why you asked me about that."

"I don't know. Just displaying my complete ignorance of the South. The only Southern state I've ever been to is Florida and what I've seen there is New York South. It's filled with nail salons and malls and New York City retirees."

Harry laughed.

"It's true," Acey said. "You were right about the *Urban Cowboy* thing. I have zero knowledge of the whole area except what I've seen on television."

"Well, my father's in ranching," Harry said.

He didn't elaborate, and Acey wanted to ask about his father's business but she hadn't the least idea what to say about ranching. She'd read a few save-the-ranch-type romance novels, but that was about it. "That must be very hard work," she finally decided to say. "I bet he doesn't stop working the entire day."

"That much," Harry said, "is true."

"And does your mother work on the ranch, too?"

Did Harry flinch? "No, not really."

"But you must ride horses, then."

"No, I don't. I…can't."

"You can't?" Why wouldn't he? "You aren't afraid of riding horses, are you?"

"Actually, I am. Hey, where are we going anyway?"

Acey stopped. She'd just instinctively walked toward her apartment building and now they were just a half block away. "I'm not sure. I didn't think our plans through. I'm notorious for that, I guess."

"For what?"

"Not following through on things. According to my family."

"What things?"

"College, for one. I dropped out because I wasn't sure what I wanted to study and it was expensive and I didn't want to waste the money."

"Makes sense to me."

"Really? I'm supposed to be regretting it."

"Do you?"

"I might do things differently now if I could, but I have to make a living now."

Harry fell silent as three things occurred to him. One, it was clear she didn't know who he was. Two, she had become the first real friend of Harry, Guy Next Door, as opposed to Harrison, Playboy Heir, and Harry liked it. Three, she was more than a little misguided about the power of money. She seemed to think money was necessary for happiness—and who better to show her it wasn't than he, the man who had learned the hard way?

A project, a plan, formed in Harry's head. He'd set out to show her the cheaper-but-finer things in life.

And that little no-women vow he'd taken? Not a problem, he told himself. Even if he was plagued by an accidental moment of weakness, Acey had made it clear she considered them only friends. So, nothing could happen.

"Are we near your place?"

Acey, arms full of travel brochures, pointed with her chin. "Yeah, right there."

"Can I see where you live? Then we can get some lunch. Unless you ate already."

Acey shook her head.

"Okay. Let's see your place, and then we'll get some grub."

"Grub," Acey repeated. "I never heard anyone say that for real. Okay," she relented. A few brochures slipped from her grip. "Here, take a few," Acey said, picking some and handing them over. "Take them home."

"I thought they were for Steph."

"Just the Greece ones," Acey said, fishing those out and handing him the rest. "The safaris are for you. So you can dream of places you've never been, and maybe make some future plans?"

A graceful giraffe peered out at Harry from the cover of one brochure. Its liquid eyes spoke to him and told him what to do next. Harry had decided to help Acey and he now knew the first thing he'd do.

Go for it, the giraffe said silently.

"Speaking of future plans, do you have any for your next day off? Saturday?" he asked. "Of course, if I'm hogging all your days off, please say so."

"Not at all," Acey said. "I enjoy…spending time with you."

Harry wondered briefly about the hesitation but let it go. "Okay. But we have to get a move on early. Can you get up and be ready by, say, nine?"

"In the *morning?*" she asked. "Oy. I can try."

"I'll swing by for you then. I have an idea."

"Can I have a hint?"

He held up the brochure and showed her the cover. She wrinkled her brow and shrugged. "What kind of hint is that?"

"That's all the hint you get," Harry said. "And, hey, you said it's not your color, but I strongly advise you to wear khaki."

Acey grinned. "Why? Why?"

"You'll see," Harry said, and they continued to walk, Acey still asking why.

"I still *cannot* believe you're seeing Harry again today," Steph said, wide-eyed. "Amazing how you've followed through on the Harry project this far. And you even brought him *here?*"

Steph was reclining on her bed, watching her older sister, clad only in a black stretch T-shirt and pink panties, rifle through dresser drawers.

"Thanks for the shaky vote of confidence," Acey said, yanking out a pair of jeans and squinting at them before tossing them on the floor. "And we just stopped in quickly before having lunch." *Because I didn't want to have that much masculine sexiness hanging around the apartment longer than five minutes.* "Can I borrow your cargo pants?"

Steph narrowed her eyes. "Why?"

Acey stopped and regarded her sister. "What do you mean, 'Why?' You always let me borrow your stuff."

"Yeah, but you hate cargo pants. You say they're boy clothes, and you prefer girl clothes."

"I just need them. Please."

Steph rolled off the bed, opened one of her own drawers and extracted the folded pants. Acey reached for them and Steph backed up a step, holding the pants over her head. "Oh, no, you don't. Not until you tell me why you want them."

"I don't want to have to kick your ass," Acey said. "But I will if you don't hand 'em over."

"I'm so not afraid of you."

Acey heaved one of her trademark sighs, but Steph was born immune. "Look, I need to wear something in khaki, and I don't have anything, so I need to borrow the pants. Happy?"

"No." But Steph handed her the pants. Acey shook them out, then tugged them over one leg, then the other. "Khaki's not really your color," Steph reminded her.

"I *know* that," Acey replied.

"Where are you going in those?"

"I have no idea." Acey sat on her bed and dumped out her makeup bag. She grabbed the concealer and dabbed it under her eyes. "Harry said to be ready at nine, and wear khaki."

"That's the weirdest thing I ever heard."

"And he showed me the Africa brochure for a hint."

Steph thought a few minutes. "Wait."

"What?"

"Maybe it worked! Maybe he's taking you over to the lottery office to claim his prize."

"And the khaki would be for…?"

"Hmm," Steph said. "Maybe he's sending you on a safari to thank you! I bet that's it. Pack a bag."

"No," Acey said, but her heart pounded. Could she have done it? Could Harry be accepting the thirty-five million? "I'm not packing anything. Even if Harry was collecting his win, I wouldn't take his money anyway. I was just doing the right thing, not going for a piece."

"I know," Steph said. "But maybe he'll insist, as a reward for helping him see the light. Take six pairs of underwear. And some bug spray."

"Stop it. I will not."

"At least bring a camera. Take mine. It's little and it will fit in your purse. You can send me pictures of lions and I can set my next book in Africa."

"How very self-serving."

Steph ran a hand under her bed, and it emerged with her camera, which she shoved at Acey. Acey made a show of dropping it into her bag. "Satisfied?"

"You'll thank me later."

"I'll only thank you for ceasing to torment me with this ridiculous idea of yours," Acey told her younger sister. "Maybe we're just going to the travel agency to get more brochures for you."

"They were useful. I'm going to slay my next victim and have his bloody corpse surface in this tourist attraction where—"

"Save the gory details," Acey said, holding up a restraining hand. "I know the characters are from your imagination, but you still give me nightmares."

"Really?" Steph asked, pleased. "That's the nicest thing you could ever say to me, Acey."

"And on that weird note," Acey said, "I'm outta here. I'm going to wait outside."

"Don't you want to invite him in? I want to meet him."

"No offense, but no, and it's not you. I don't want him to get the wrong idea. I still need a little time to make Mr. Millionaire come around to his new fortune, and I don't want him to run for cover from what he thinks is a crazy single girl on the prowl."

"Oh, all right." Steph pouted. "Can I at least peek out the window?"

"If you promise to be sneaky about it." She turned in a slow circle. "How do I look?"

"About as good as you could in those pants, but," Steph asked, "why do you care? Like you said, you don't want to look like a crazy single girl on the prowl. Unless…"

"Unless what?"

"Unless you do."

Acey stood still for a moment, then turned to her dresser. She whipped a tissue out of a box and vigorously wiped her lips free of the gloss she'd carefully applied fifteen minutes earlier. "There," she declared. "No conflict of interest from me. Just a man and a mission."

"Is that me you're trying to convince?"

Acey stuck out her tongue and flounced from the room. Little sisters thought they were so smart. She slammed out the front door and stuffed her keys into her purse next to her wallet. Her spending cash for the week was tucked inside, just in case.

Who knew where she'd end up today?

Chapter Six

The elephant swung his trunk back and forth, back and forth, as if trying to decide, out of everything in the world, what to do next. He dipped the tip of his trunk into a brownish puddle by his massive feet and flipped it up to splash the water across his face. Acey clicked the shutter just as he did it, and hoped the photo would capture the droplets hurling toward his warm, wrinkled face, and the brief expression of relief on his ancient features.

As if reading her mind, Harry whispered in her ear, "That'll be a good one."

Acey, smiling wide, nodded. "It's so amazing," she breathed. "He's such an incredible creature and, in the real world, I'd never encounter him. But here he is, and here I am, and it's…" Her words trailed off.

"I know what you mean," Harry said. "It's a magical experience. Worth far more than the price of admission, I'd venture to say."

Acey turned to Harry then, and they shared a grin before she shoved Steph's camera back into her purse. From somewhere in the near distance, a wild, unidentifiable bird cried out, and Acey closed her eyes, finding it extremely easy to pretend she was on safari in Africa, and not just at the African animals section of the Bronx Zoo.

"How are you liking our wild adventure so far?" Harry asked, gently tugging Acey's elbow. She opened her eyes and allowed herself to be led from the elephant.

"Full of danger at every turn," she said, "but I'm confident I can handle it."

"That's good, because we're about to encounter the most dangerous part of our safari. Many an explorer has come this far, only to fail to make it out alive."

"Not me. I'm ready for anything."

"I certainly hope so, because we are now approaching—" Harry dragged out the suspense "—the snack-bar line."

"Oh, no!" Acey cried in mock terror. "Not the snack line!"

"Oh, yes. Pushing, shoving, scorching sunlight, thirsty people griping at each other, children wailing for ice-cream cones. If you can survive this, you can survive anything."

"Maybe you'd better hold my hand," Acey blurted in the spirit of their joke, then wanted to bite back the words.

Harry grasped her hand and squeezed her fingers, letting his own shake a little bit as if in fear. Or maybe that was her hand shaking in very real fear. Acey couldn't tell, so she didn't laugh.

Harry had been right about one thing. This was the most dangerous part of the day so far.

"Nice pants," Harry said.

"Thanks," Acey said. "I had to go through a lot to get them."

"The effort is appreciated. What's your favorite animal so far?"

Acey thought for a moment, grateful for the question to distract her from her palm, sweating into Harry's. "I think I liked the lions best. They remind me so much of Sherlock, my cat. Their movements are the same. The way they twitch their ears, flick their tails, lie down for a nap. And the I'm-better-than-any-other-beast expression."

Harry laughed. "I liked them, too." He thought a moment. "If you think about it, it really is an honor to have a pet. For an animal to allow you to get so close, and to trust you."

"That's a nice way to put it," Acey said. "I'll have to remember that the next time Sherlock stands on my bladder in the morning to wake me up for his breakfast." She expected Harry to laugh again, but he was just staring straight ahead of them. A running child's yellow balloon bumped the side of his head lightly, but he didn't react. "Harry?"

"Huh?"

"Earth to Harry?"

"Oh, I'm—" He slid his hand from hers and unnecessarily smoothed his hair. "I'm sorry. I was…just… thinking."

Acey realized that even after spending lots of time

this week with Harry, he was still largely a mystery. "You spaced out when we were talking about pets. Did it make you think of a pet you used to have?"

"I—" Harry began, and stopped. He swallowed and it seemed to take a great deal of effort for him to start again. "Can't get anything by you, can I?" He gave her an empty smile. "Yeah, I was thinking about an animal I used to…kind of have."

"It died?"

"Yes." Then Harry quieted, apparently unwilling to divulge any more information.

Acey supposed the reaction arose from resurfaced grief, and she sympathized. "I'm sorry. It's very hard to lose an animal. Especially one you got to know very well. Sherlock's surly and unfriendly, but if anything happened to him, he is a family member."

She half expected Harry to open up a little, tell her more about his pet, the circumstances of its passing, maybe even just whether it was a cat or a dog or hamster, but he said nothing. Acey guessed the loss was recent, considering the wound had obviously not yet healed.

The pimply-faced teen behind the snack-bar counter said, "Next?" in a tone that implied Acey and Harry hadn't paid attention the first time she'd said it.

Harry allowed Acey to order first, and by the time he counted out his money, he was beginning to sound normal again, bouncing back from the flash of anguish. Acey tried to hand the cashier a ten-dollar bill, but Harry pushed it back at her. "Your money's no good here."

"Yes, it is, take it."

"Nope. You insisted we split the admission and I let

you win on that one, but I invited you here, so I want to pay for something."

"No."

Harry ignored her, picked up the tray with their hot dogs and sodas and carried it to a picnic table. Acey followed him. "I want to pay for my lunch," she said to the back of his blue polo shirt.

"Too bad," he said over his shoulder, spreading their food out on the table.

Acey clenched her teeth. "Take my money or I'm going home."

That made Harry turn around. "Why? I thought we were having fun."

"We were. We are." Acey tried to keep her voice strong and even but heard it crack in desperation. "Just take it."

She thrust the ten at him and he took it, baffled. He gave her a few dollars in change and sat down across from her. Her face was flushed hot from her insistence, so she took a long drink of soda to try to cool off.

"Honey," Harry said, "I think y'all are getting a helluva sunburn on your face."

Acey burned even hotter at the endearment, then told herself they probably all called each other "honey" in the friendlier South. "I don't have a sunburn."

"You're okay," Harry said, and Acey exhaled. "Didn't I say only the strong survive the snack line?" he added. "It got pretty hairy there for both of us, but we did it."

Acey eased her stiffened shoulders.

"Now that the literal heat of the moment has passed," Harry said, "I sincerely apologize for not understanding how important it is to you to pay your own way. If you don't mind my asking, why *is* it so important?"

Acey stared down at her hot dog, which was oozing mustard into the cardboard tray. "I don't like men to buy me things. I work for a living."

She peeked up and saw Harry take a bite of his own hot dog. He chewed, swallowed, then said, "Might this have anything to do with your old boyfriend?"

Acey froze. "What?"

"It just seems like the kind of proclamation a woman makes after she's been done wrong."

Acey took her own bite so as to fill her mouth with something other than words.

"Spill it," Harry commanded.

Acey swallowed down an ice-filled gulp too fast and hiccuped. "Excuse me," she said. "Although, come to think of it, it's the perfect lead-in to a story about a guy who turns my stomach. I broke up with Charlie a year ago."

"After how long?"

"A year. I met him at a bar in Greenwich Village. I was there helping a friend celebrate her birthday and this icky guy kept hitting on me. Charlie stepped in and pretended he was my date who'd just arrived so this guy would back off."

"Slick move."

"Yeah, it was, and I was appreciative, so even though I didn't think Charlie Stone was exactly my type, I agreed to go out with him. The next week he came here to Long Island, let me choose a restaurant, bought me dinner and we had a great talk. I liked him. I was flattered he liked me, to be honest."

"That's crazy. Every man who passes by stares at you."

"Oh, stop." Acey felt herself growing warm again, and this time, it wasn't her face.

"It's true. I'm a man. I notice these things. Tell me why you were flattered."

"He was really educated," Acey said, recovering. "He had two master's degrees from different Ivy League schools. And he was *wealthy*."

"Why is that flattering?" Harry said, and she noticed his eyebrow twitch as he asked.

Remembering she was talking to a newly rich guy, she chose her words carefully. "I didn't care about it one way or another, but a lot of women do like rich men, so when he chose to keep dating me, I thought this must mean he thought I was special."

"What did he do, to have all this money?"

"Uh, he got born to rich parents."

"Ah."

"He didn't do anything for a living, despite all his education. If anyone asked, he said he was a consultant, but that was just a word. And I wasn't thinking about all that at first. He took me to places I'd read about. New clubs, fancy restaurants, surprise weekend getaways."

Harry was starting to feel itchy. It was as if Acey had dated Harry himself. He wondered just how many women out there were, at this moment, telling the same version of the Charlie story, except to them, it was the Harrison story. He could see she was leading up to an unhappy ending, and he had a sinking feeling he'd experience the guilt that should have been Charlie's alone.

"He never let me pay for a thing," Acey said. "I was a little uncomfortable with it all but I stayed with him. I thought he couldn't help being rich any more than I couldn't help *not* being rich.

"Long story short," she said. "One day he took me to his parents' summer home in the Hamptons. I met Mr.

and Mrs. Stone, who were very gracious and welcoming. To my face."

"Uh-oh."

"Yeah. I went off to find the bathroom, and when I got lost in their big house, I circled back to the dining room. They didn't expect me back so quickly, and didn't hear me on their four-inch-thick carpet. I caught his mother saying that I obviously had nothing in common with him and I was clearly just after his money."

Harry's heart ached. "That must have been hard."

"It was. Especially when she called me 'that little pizza girl.' Can you believe that?"

Harry couldn't.

"But I rationalized," Acey went on. "You can't control your parents, and just because they were jerks didn't mean he was, too."

"Very generous of you, considering the insult."

"Maybe, but I thought—" she said, and stopped. She took her last bite of hot dog, chewed very slowly and swallowed. It took her another half minute to restart her story. "I thought Charlie loved me. Three days later, I went to a party one of his friends was hosting. Again, I walked away to get a drink, and when I came back I overheard the conversation. But this time it was all him. His friends were saying disgusting frat-boy-type things about me, and Charlie said, 'Yeah, and she's hot in bed, so I think I'll slum around with her a little while longer.'"

Harry's emotions threatened to eat him from the inside out. He hurt, because the kind of man she'd been hurt by was like the kind of men he'd surrounded himself with most of his life—college roommates, sons of his father's business associates. He knew how they operated, on levels even Acey would never know. He'd only begun to shy away from those types of friends when he'd made acquaintance with kind, earnest Wayne, and then had cut them out completely when he'd left Texas.

"I broke up with the dirtbag on the spot," Acey said. "He ran after me out to the street and begged me to stay. He offered to take me to Paris. Goddamn *Paris,* to make up for what I'd just heard. Like money could possibly fix everything."

Harry heard Acey's words, but they had begun to swirl with another woman's words inside his brain, mentally mixing into a poisonous brew. *"Harry,"* Lara had said. *"You think money can solve everything, don't you? Always your answer. Belle, my beautiful horse, is dead, because of you! And your solution is to just buy me another one? I loved Belle, and now she's gone, and it's your fault. I'll never forgive you."*

"That was the only way he knew how," Harry heard himself say.

"What?" Acey asked.

"Charlie." Harry's focus was locked on a knot in the wood picnic table. "Money was all he ever had to back him up, his lifelong ace in the hole, so he pulled it out to try to keep you."

The space that was usually filled with Acey's cute New Yorkese was filled instead with silence, and stretched out so long that Harry was able to tear his eyes off the table. He saw Acey, heard her blowing breath hard in and out through her nostrils.

"Huh," Acey finally said. She was holding her paper cup so tightly that it looked like it might collapse in her grip. "You know, I've told a few people this story—men *and* women, incidentally—and never before has someone tried to make me see the light of Charlie's actions. The general reaction has been of outrage on my behalf. So thank you for giving me that much-needed perspective. I'll be sure to meditate on it."

Harry could have kicked himself. "Acey, I didn't mean that the way it came out. I'm trying to figure how any man could feel so entitled to you, or your love and attention—"

"You don't have to—" Acey cut in, but Harry countered with his own interruption.

"I'm not finished. Charlie had no right to treat you badly, behind your back or to your face. He was the lucky one in your relationship, not you. That rich guy should have realized—and maybe one day, in hindsight, he did—that he only came into real wealth the day he met you."

The words enthusiastically tumbled from his lips before he could censor them or perhaps ease them out with a little less fervor. Acey sat frozen, appearing too stunned to respond.

"The saddest thing," Harry added, "is you won't ever again let a well-meaning man pay for your lunch."

"Oh, sorry. I guess that's the reason you heard this story in the first place, huh? I guess the whole thing has soured me on letting someone take care of me. I believed, and still do a bit, that if I hadn't been caught up in his world of money and fun, that I might have seen his true colors sooner."

"Not necessarily."

"No, not necessarily, but why take any chances?"

"Surely all rich men aren't bad."

"No," Acey said slowly. "Not all. Maybe some

men—people—who come from modest backgrounds and then come into a lot of money can—possibly—appreciate its value more. For example, people who work very hard to advance in business or people who suddenly get a…a windfall."

"Like, for example, the mysterious lottery winner?"

Acey choked on her soda. Hard. An ice sliver flew out of her mouth and landed on the table between them. Harry jumped up and eased behind her to thump her on the back. When, between coughs, she managed, "I'm fine, I'm fine," he stayed right where he was, rubbing her upper back. The hot sun behind her had dampened her stretchy T-shirt with perspiration, just enough for Harry to feel as though he was sliding his hand up and down her bare skin. His palm dragged over each delicate vertebra of her spine. He didn't notice when she stopped coughing.

When Acey had composed herself enough to pick up their conversation, she didn't turn to face Harry. Instead, she addressed the spot he had been sitting in a few moments ago. "Yes, like the lottery winner. Hopefully he or, um, she, will do the right things with all those millions and not use them carelessly. In fact, I know he will. I have faith." She completed the sentence with a sharp nod for a period.

A few moments ticked by. "So," Harry said, reluctantly giving up the back rub and, unable to sever the contact, dropping both hands onto her shoulders. "As for men born with the stereotypical silver spoon?"

"Those people," Acey practically spit, "have no clue what it's like to be without, have no idea how to relate to the majority of the world. In their minds, they're princes who deserve everything they desire because they can flash a gold card. But the truth is," she said, turning around to make her point to Harry's face, "the only thing they deserve is a loud, nasty wake-up call."

Looking at Acey, anguish for long-ago wrongs torturing her brow, Harry was tempted to confess his truth. Instead, he said, "I couldn't agree more."

Acey nodded once and turned back to the table. Harry came around her and began to clear their lunch remains. "Get out that zoo map," he commanded. "Where are we headed next?"

"Let's see," Acey said, fumbling with the colored paper, and Harry could hear her relief. "Oh! Monkeys."

"Good. I'm in the mood for monkeys."

"Whoever isn't?"

"Good point." He hesitated only a moment to offer his arm, and Acey hesitated only a moment to take it. They strolled from the picnic area, and the sun on Harry's neck wasn't nearly as warm as the new heat on the inside of his elbow.

The trip to the zoo had taken some time on public transportation, requiring train and bus trips, so by the time Acey and Harry returned to Valley Stream, the last of the blue sky was streaking away into gold, already transforming the present day into a recent memory.

"How do you rate our day with the animals?" Harry asked.

"Hmm," Acey replied. "I'd have to say ten out of ten. No, make that a nine out of ten. The lunch discussion was on the heavy side."

"Agreed," Harry said. A pause, then, "It was almost ten out of ten, huh? A ten being the all-time pinnacle of funness?"

"You got it."

"I'm wondering then. If you were on a real safari, and the fun scale still only went to ten, then it would rank pretty close to today. *Don't you think?*"

Would you be on that safari with me? Acey thought. *Because if you weren't, then it probably wouldn't touch today.* She couldn't say that out loud though, so she went with an intelligent-sounding "uh-huh."

Harry said nothing.

"Your point being?" Acey asked, exasperated.

"My point being," Harry explained, "that we saved literally thousands of dollars in travel expenses and malaria-immunization fees and we had a great day all the same."

Acey raised an eyebrow. Okay, what was this about? "Yes, we did. Still, are you suggesting today was comparable to taking an exotic trip to a faraway land?"

"I would never suggest you ought to believe anything I believe. You're a woman with strong opinions."

"You got that right."

"So I'm merely suggesting you *consider* the crazy idea that today *was* comparable."

It was Acey's turn to fall silent, and her mind replayed a quick montage of the day. She and Harry doubled over with laughter at a somersaulting baby monkey. She and Harry watching a lion sleep for about a half hour, even though it was clear the big cat wasn't planning on moving from his sunny spot for hours. Harry buying her lemonade when she wasn't looking and her letting him, then wiping her condensation-covered hands on his shirt as payment. Harry's fingers on her shoulders, rubbing her back. His scent of clean cotton and something else, something rugged and manly that she just couldn't…

Ahem. *Ahem.* "I will," Acey said slowly, "consider it."

"Excellent. Make sure y'all get back to me."

Yup. As soon as I can forget the feel of your hands on my spine, I will get right back to you.

"You know what I need right now?"

A cold shower? Acey guessed to herself. No, that was just her. "What?"

"Some bread. And, come to think of it, milk."

"Oh, good idea," Acey said. "Steph made the last few convenience-store runs. I haven't seen Rosalia since… around the time I first saw, ah, you."

Luckily, they reached the door to Bread and Milk at that moment, effectively cutting off any opportunity to reminisce about that first electrically charged meeting.

The door was propped open, as usual, and the air inside was even hotter and stuffier than it had been outside at noon. The warm air coaxed out different smells—doughnuts in boxes, tobacco from behind the counter, minty candy. It wasn't long until closing, and there were no customers, and Rosalia was watching a tiny black-and-white television propped on a stool near the register. George Costanza was waving his arms at Jerry Seinfeld. Rosalia was chuckling.

"*Hola!*" Acey called cheerily, and Rosalia turned her head.

"Acey!" she cried. "And—nice young man!" Rosalia widened her eyes at Acey, but it was quick and subtle.

"This is Harry, but you know him," Acey said. "You just didn't know his name."

"So many people here like that," Rosalia said by way of apology. Harry waved it off with a grin.

"Very interesting that…you and Harry are both here," Rosalia said, obviously being careful about her wording.

"Not that interesting," Harry laughed. "I need a few things. If you ladies will excuse me."

He disappeared down an aisle and Rosalia took hold of Acey's shirtsleeve. "You didn't come in after last time. I thought, eh, she's busy. She'll tell me next time what she thinks. But I see, you are busy with Harry."

"Rosalia, I have to be honest, I think he *is* the one."

"Ah, this I have wanted to hear!" Rosalia clasped her hands over a red heart embroidered on her diaphanous white shirt. "It is exactly as I hoped. I am so happy!"

"You should be. It's all your doing. All you had to do was point me in the right direction."

"I knew that. I am smart." She tapped her forehead with one finger.

Acey giggled. "You sure are. And I was hoping the same as you. He's so sweet to everyone. He deserves the best."

"And now he has it," Rosalia said, laying a hand on Acey's head affectionately.

"The only thing is," Acey said, watching Harry as he moved between aisles, "he is a hard nut to crack."

"What do you mean?"

"I mean, it's going to take a little convincing. Actually, a lot of convincing."

"What? No, that can't be right," Rosalia said.

Harry loudly cleared his throat, and both women looked up in time to catch him juggling three oranges. Acey clapped.

"You see that? He likes you," Rosalia said, lowering her voice. "Men do silly things only for women they like."

"Yeah, well," Acey was now whispering, too. "Unfortunately, liking me has nothing to do with collecting thirty-five million dollars."

"What?" Rosalia dropped her hands to her slender hips. "Acey, you are saying what?"

"You know what I'm saying. I can't get Harry to admit he won the money. I'm working on it."

Rosalia was silent for a moment. "He told you he did not win?" she finally asked.

"No. But he didn't tell me he *did* win. Not yet."

"Oh, Acey, that is..." Rosalia's voice trailed off. "That is a shame. I thought you and he—"

Harry stepped up to the counter and dropped a loaf of bread, a container of milk, two lemonades and a package of Twinkies on the counter. Rosalia rang up his items, pausing once to give Acey a look she couldn't interpret.

"Didn't get enough junk food at the zoo?" Acey asked Harry.

"This is tomorrow's junk food."

Rosalia accepted his money and made change. She was still quiet, and Acey wasn't sure why.

"Bye, Rosalia," Harry said. "Nice to see you again."

"And you, of course," Rosalia answered. "You go ahead, while I have quick girl talk with Acey."

He ambled out, and Acey regarded her friend quizzically.

"I wonder if you are missing the big picture," Rosalia said.

"What could be a bigger picture than thirty-five million dollars?" Acey asked. "I'm doing the best I can here."

"Maybe I mean, you need to stand back and look at him closer than you are looking at him now."

Acey sighed. "Harry considers money to be evil and

corrupting. I'm sure he's the winner, and he's afraid of it."

"Acey, Acey," Rosalia said. "Are you sure you're not the one who is afraid?"

Acey struggled with comprehension.

"Okay," Rosalia said. "You go with Harry. Find out the truth, and do with it what your heart tells you. This you promise?"

"Of course." Acey would have asked Rosalia to elaborate, but a teenage couple came in, followed by an elderly man. "You take care."

"Come in soon. *With* Harry."

Acey left the store, and the first thing she felt was a newly cooled breeze on her cheek. Harry was a few feet away from her, playing with a Labrador puppy one of the new customers had left leashed to a parking meter. He didn't see Acey, and she took the moment to clear her mind.

Rosalia's words had confused her. Hadn't she requested Acey check Harry out in the first place? What was she suggesting Acey was afraid of? Finding out the truth? Acey'd told Rosalia she was trying. What else could she do?

Although, come to think of it, she hadn't tried very hard today. She'd allowed Harry to lead her around, and she'd told Harry some big long story about her own last relationship, and hadn't made the slightest bit of progress on the whole lottery thing, if Harry's talk about cheap zoo versus pricy safari was any indication.

One thing was true though: It *had* been a fun day. More fun than she'd had in an awfully long time. It would be hard to pretend that money would have made it any better.

"Y'all about ready to go?" Harry drawled in her ear, and Acey, caught in a reverie, jumped.

"Here's where we probably should part ways."

"I'd be no gentleman if I didn't see you to your door."

"All right then."

They strolled the short route to Acey's, neither saying much, comfortable in the reticence that often follows a long day of talking.

When they got to the front door of Acey's building, she swiveled around to face him.

If this was a date, Acey thought, *this would be the moment we would kiss.* But this wasn't, and this wouldn't be.

She was afraid to stare at his lips in the universal sign of permission. She forced herself to smile with her own lips stretched thin, tight and unapproachable. Very difficult, considering her libido was screaming at her to do the opposite.

Acey, her mind chastised, *kissing and related activities are not part of the plan. The plan is the priority. Follow through.*

"Good night, Harry," she heard herself say.

"Good…good night, Acey," Harry replied, and for the first time Acey could recall, he didn't sound one-hundred-percent confident. "Uh, wait. Here," he said, rummaging in his pocket for the crumpled zoo map. "Got a pen?"

Acey fished one out of her bag and Harry scribbled on the map. "Here you are," he said. "My phone number. I just realized you didn't have it."

It shouldn't have seemed so awkward to take his number after the whole day, but it somehow was. "Th-thank you," Acey stammered.

He turned and walked away from her, down the walkway and to the street. He turned back once, and Acey swirled around quickly and pretended to fumble with her keys. When she pushed on the door, she looked over her shoulder, expecting to see no one. Harry hadn't moved. He lifted his arm, as if to wave, but he just held up his hand, his palm facing her. She mirrored the gesture and walked into her building. She closed the door and leaned her back against it, breathing through her mouth.

Acey was fast realizing that being with Harry was becoming more and more of a challenge. She hadn't gotten far with her plan today, she thought again, but she was going to have to kick it up a notch. Maybe more for her sake than his, at this point. She feared losing her senses if she hung around him much longer. She was going to fast-track him to that money, so she could fast-track herself away from him. Acey lifted her chin in resolution.

Harry Wells was about to get a healthy dose of tough love.

Love?

His feet should have been tired from the day, but as Harry headed to his own small apartment, he had to fight the urge to Gene Kelly his way up the nearest lamppost.

I'm getting to you, Acey Corelli, he sang to a big-band tune in his mind. Miss Money Talks was breaking. He hadn't known what hit him in the travel agency, but he had made a strong showing in round two at the zoo. Hopefully, Acey would soon concede that money wasn't necessary to have the nicest things in life.

It hadn't escaped Harry's attention that Acey was an

unusual dichotomy. On the one hand, she talked about how money had made her ex—whom Harry would have enjoyed being alone with for about three minutes—grow up into the devil incarnate, and on the other hand, she enjoyed chattering about how money would make Harry's life easier and more fun. Something didn't make sense.

Well, money was a complex thing, Harry concluded. Maybe everyone was conflicted about it. He certainly had been.

He'd seen Acey's face, though, when he asked her to rate the zoo trip. He was getting to her.

As much as she was getting to him? He felt the sudden need to readjust himself in his jeans, but being out in plain sight, he resisted the urge.

Project Acey, he reminded himself. His biggest challenge so far, one he was sure to love.

Love?

Chapter Seven

"There you go."

The woman inhaled the tantalizing garlicky cheese scent. "Mmm. This is the high point of my week," she said. "Of course, the low point of my week will come in fifteen minutes, when I start thinking about what this will do to my thighs."

Acey laughed. "If I had a dollar for every woman who comes in here and says that," she replied, "well, I'd probably spend it on pizza."

The woman laughed with her.

"Just enjoy it," Acey said. "You only live once."

The woman carried her tray to a table and sat, taking an immediate bite of one slice. Then she pulled a sheaf of papers from a black portfolio and spread them out next to her food. Acey wondered where the woman worked. She guessed this was a woman who commanded respect from her colleagues. Acey looked down at her sauce-smeared apron with disgust, just as one of her own "colleagues" said, "Can you grab the next customer?"

"We're clear right now," Acey told Lydia, who was staring at the mute television mounted near the ceiling.

On-screen, a beautiful blonde and a chiseled, shirtless and needlessly oiled-up stud were having a heated discussion. "How can you follow that with the sound down?"

"It's almost impossible," Lydia said, not taking her eyes off the drama, "but Dad said not to turn it up."

"What's going on in this story?" Acey asked, since there was not much else for her to do at the moment.

"Well, Dirk, that's the guy…"

"And I would never have guessed that perspiring guy could have such a sensible name as Dirk," Acey said.

The sarcasm went over Lydia's head. "That's Alexandria, his ex-lover who just recovered from amnesia, and she just found out that while she was in a coma from the cruise-ship collision, he was getting it on with her half sister."

"That's kind of harsh."

"She *was* in a coma for a long time," Lydia said reasonably.

Acey passed a damp rag over the crumb-covered glass counter, and nearly jumped as Lydia emitted a loud gasp. Acey looked up in time to catch the blue-and-white breaking-news banner splashed across the screen.

"Crap!" Lydia cried. "It's bad enough I have to try to read lips to keep up with my damn show. Now it's interrupted by something I bet isn't even important."

Acey grinned and went back to wiping the counter while Lydia cursed again.

When Acey heard Lydia say behind her, "Oh. Wow," she tried to ignore it. She was distracted enough these days. She didn't want to get into the habit of watching television on her shift.

She didn't realize Anthony had come away from the ovens to the front until she heard him say close to her, "Hey, check it out. That millionaire finally stepped forward."

Acey whirled, dropping the rag on her feet with a soft sploosh. She squinted at the TV.

A brunette reporter in a smart red jacket was doing a stand-up. The graphic underneath her read, "Thirty-five-million-dollar lottery jackpot winner comes forward."

"Turn that up!" Acey shrieked, rummaging under the counter in a desperate search for the remote.

"Dad said not to," Lydia began, but she obviously saw something in Acey's expression that stopped her argument cold. "Ah, screw it. Here it is." She tossed the remote to Acey, who caught it in her left hand and turned the volume up as loud as it would go so it could be heard over the radio.

"...name has not been revealed," the reporter was saying. "All we know at this point is that it is a man approximately in his early thirties, who is a resident of Valley Stream, where the winning ticket was purchased nearly two weeks ago."

Acey's brain cells began to tumble over one another in a mad scramble to process the information they were receiving. Early thirties. Valley Stream resident... Oh, God. Oh, *God.*

Her zoo trip with Harry had been only the day before yesterday, and she hadn't seen or spoken to him since. She'd thought about him something like a zillion times, but that was irrelevant.

Had she said the perfect thing to Harry at the zoo and not realized it? What could it have been?

The reporter was outside the lottery office in Albany, and was repeating the same information over and over. Early thirties, Valley Stream resident, arrived unaccompanied shortly after the lottery office opened this morning.

The network finally took pity on the floundering reporter and cut back to the studio, where the anchorman instructed viewers to tune in to the evening edition, when they expected to reveal the winner's name and other news.

Dirk and Alexandria resumed their argument.

"Amazing," Anthony said. Two male customers who'd just come in nodded. "I wonder if I know the guy."

"I doubt it," Lydia said. "*Your* stupid friends don't have the brains to pick six numbers. Not even if they all worked together."

Acey still had Harry's phone number in her wallet. She'd slipped it in there Saturday night, and although she'd inexplicably pulled it out several times in the past thirty-six hours to pass her finger over his handwriting, she hadn't dialed it.

If she dialed it now, he—theoretically—should be at home working on a grant letter. No reason why he wouldn't answer the phone. Unless he just *happened* to be at the lottery office. Collecting.

Acey walked over to the coat closet, which held no

coats at this warm time of year, just old brooms and buckets. She retrieved her purse from the top shelf where she usually stashed it and yanked it open. Her fingernails ran over the roughed-up leather of her brown wallet and she pulled it out. She unzipped the middle compartment and withdrew the phone number gingerly. She stared at it for the billionth time, noticing again the squashed top curve of both eights, and the loopless, flat-bottomed two. She pinched the corner of the paper scrap between her fingers and carried it to the phone. She'd memorized the digital sequence by now, but as she lifted the receiver and began to dial, she looked at each number in turn, to make sure she was correct.

"Who ya callin'?" Anthony asked, as if Acey's business was suddenly his business.

"I'm calling for pizza," Acey said. "What do you want on it?"

"Very funny," Anthony said, and went back to the oven. Acey rolled her eyes and finished dialing. Then she held her breath and waited.

She realized too late she should have formulated a reason for calling, in case Harry did answer, but in her heart, Acey had a feeling she wouldn't have to bother. Then that hopeful feeling was replaced by a sour one: If he was in Albany, and she'd done her job, would she ever see him again?

One ring, two rings, three rings.

I did this for him, Acey said to herself. *I had to.*

But she hadn't considered, until now, how Harry the New Millionaire might not have time for a new old friend.

Four rings, five rings, six rings.

Each ring hurt Acey a little more.

* * *

"Wayne, can I call you back tonight? I want to talk to you, buddy, but I have a lot of work to catch up on."

"First time I ever heard y'all say something like that."

Harry laughed. "That's probably true. Well, I suppose work waited all my life, so it can wait another five minutes. How you doin'?"

Wayne laughed, too. "How you doin'?" he repeated. "What a New Yorker. Hey, I think your call-waiting's going."

"Ignore it. Whoever it is can call back."

Acey replaced the receiver, stunned. She shouldn't have been stunned, but there it was. Harry wasn't home.

Her fingers were still on the phone when it rang, nearly causing her to jump out the window. She picked it up before the ring was complete. "Hello? I mean, uh, yeah, hello. Focaccia's. Can I help you?"

"Acey?" Steph's voice filled her ear. "Why do you sound so weird? I've been trying to call you. Did you see the news?"

"Yeah."

"I'm at work. I saw it on the TV here. Early thirties? Valley Stream guy? Sounds like Harry to me. Guess we'll have to wait until tonight's news to find out, unless… Hey, I know. You've got his number. Call him."

"I just…" Acey was having a hard time finishing a sentence, specifically this sentence. "I just did. He's not home."

Steph gasped.

"He *should* be home," Acey said needlessly, "but he's *not* home."

"That's great news. Isn't it?"

Acey didn't answer.

"Acey? Listen," her sister said. "Call him back, all right? You were excited and nervous, and maybe you got the number wrong. Try again."

Steph's voice had softened, and Acey realized her sister understood.

"Okay," Acey said. "I'll try again."

"I'll see you in a couple of hours."

Steph hung up and Acey lifted the phone again.

"Who ya callin'?" Lydia asked.

Stress took hold of Acey's personality and twisted it into an unrecognizable shape. "Nobody!" she yelled at the top of her lungs.

Everyone in Focaccia's turned to look at her. Lydia's eyes were wide.

"Oh, my God, Lydia," Acey said. "I'm so, so sorry. I am a total psycho."

"Yeah, you are," Lydia agreed. "And ya know, it's about time you got psycho over the right guy. That Charlie wasn't worth squat. But that cowboy? *Hello*." She put a cool hand on Acey's shoulder, and Acey squeezed it gratefully.

"*What* cowboy?" Anthony demanded.

"Wouldn't you love to know?" Lydia taunted, and their voices faded into the background as they moved away from Acey, who dialed the phone again.

"So what about that gal y'all were telling me about last time?" Wayne asked.

"Huh?"

"That woman who was, you know, hanging around you all the time, asking questions? The one you thought was a P.I.?"

"Acey." Just saying her name affected Harry. He could still smell her hair as if she was sitting right next to him.

"That must be the one. So is this Stacey a detective or what?"

"It's not Stacey, it's Acey. And no, she's not a detective. She works at a pizza place."

"She can cook, too, huh? Sounds like Harry Wells is back in business. Monkey business, that is." Wayne chuckled.

"I swear, Wayne. I told you I'm not touching another woman. Not for a good long time." Harry was silently discounting the way his hands ran over Acey's warm back less than two days ago.

"I hear clicking again. Someone must really need to reach you."

"Like who? No one calls me here other than you, and people I'm working for, and…" Acey! Harry almost slapped his own forehead. He'd just given Acey this number. Maybe she really needed him for something important, judging by the number of clicks. "Actually, you're right, I'd better get that. Take care."

Wayne said goodbye and Harry held the phone away from his ear, trying to discern which button to hit to get call-waiting. He got so few calls on this phone that no two people were ever trying to call him at the same time. He guessed the flash button, which turned out to be right. "Hello?"

"Oh, um," he heard on the other end, and recognized the delicate stammer. His mouth relaxed into a smile.

"Acey?"

"Yeah, um, hello! Harry. I just thought I'd call. To, ah, see how you're doing."

"Oh."

Pause. "How you doin', then?"

"I'm fine," Harry answered. "Did the phone ring a thousand times?"

"Kind of," Acey admitted.

"I was—" Harry began, and stopped. Maybe it was best not to tell her he was on the phone with Wayne, because it would invite questions about his family, which he didn't want. "I just got in, and I heard the phone ring awhile before I could get to it."

"Aren't you supposed to be working?"

"I am," Harry said slowly, not wanting to compound his lie with more lies. Better to just evade. "I mean, I was. I needed a little break. You know how it is."

"Right." There was an awkward pause, made all the more awkward by the mutual memory of sharing so much personal information the last time they'd been together. "I gotta go," she said. "About thirty-eight people just walked in. I'll call you, um, soon. Is that all right?"

Her last words sounded less like a tacked-on formality and more like a real question. "Of course, it's all right," Harry assured her, confused.

"Okay, bye," she said, and there was a clatter, followed by silence.

Harry hung up, but not without a nagging uneasiness. Lying was not on his to-do list for the new Harry Wells. Especially lying to Acey Corelli.

She had sounded pretty distracted, he consoled himself as he headed back to his desk and his work. Hopefully, distracted enough to let a little lie slide.

"He was lying."

"How could you tell?" Steph asked, spearing a tomato slice and cramming it into her mouth.

"It wasn't difficult," Acey said, pouring dressing over her own salad. Her sister made a mean salad, if such a thing could be said to truly exist. "He was all hedgy and evasive. I asked where he'd been, in a completely non-invasive, innocently curious way, of course."

"Of course."

"And he clammed up. 'I needed a little break.' Come on."

"That is pretty lame."

Acey swished the fork around lettuce leaves until she located a garlic crouton, which she picked out with her long fingernails. "At any rate, I've probably had my last conversation with Harry Wells," she said, crunching down on the crouton. "After tonight, when all of New York learns his name, he'll be swept away on a tide of pink champagne and thousand-dollar bills."

Acey had planned to be cavalier and joke about the whole thing, but her voice caught on the last word, and she realized she couldn't. She threw down her fork.

"Hey," Steph said, and her gentle tone made Acey look up. "This was never about you. You decided to do a wonderful thing for someone you consider a wonderful man. Wasn't it worth it?"

Acey nodded, blinking away unexpected moisture in the corners of her eyes.

"Don't jump to conclusions, Acey. I'm sure Harry wouldn't—couldn't—forget you. How could he? You made him understand he should come forward and claim his new life."

"I still don't even know how I did it," Acey mumbled. "Not that it matters now." Nothing constituted a good deed unless it included some kind of sacrifice, Acey told herself. Time or donations or whatever. In this case, a new friendship was the sacrifice. *It was worth it, it was worth it, it was worth it.*

"It's after ten," Steph pointed out, carrying her bowl to the sink and flinging it in. "I'll do the dishes later. Let's go get this over with."

Both women had missed the six-o'clock news: Acey because of dinner rush, and Steph because she was asked to work a couple of extra hours. Steph headed to the living room to flip on the television as Acey tried to control her thumping heart. She wondered if Harry's eyes would sparkle on television the way they did in person, and wondered if he'd say something like, "I just want to thank y'all for this big prize."

And she wondered if she'd be able to sit through it without breaking down.

She planted herself on the sofa next to her sister, who patted her hand as the international crises reports droned on. Steph didn't even have her notebook handy. This evening's edition of the news was different.

Finally, the anchor wrapped up the day's more serious news, and said, "And now, a con man tries, and fails, to collect a so-far unclaimed thirty-five-million-dollar lottery win."

Two Corelli jaws dropped.

The report continued. Apparently, some schmo from Valley Stream had attempted a scam, a faked ticket or something. Acey stopped listening to the actual story to concentrate on the video of a man being led away from the lottery office in cuffs. A guy in scuffed-up sneakers and hair that appeared to be going into its fourth day without a washing.

Certainly not Harry Wells.

The report concluded with a cheery "The real lottery winner remains a mystery."

Steph muted the set. "If you don't mind my saying so, holy crap."

Elation flooded through Acey, starting from the top of her head and working down to her feet before winding back up again and settling somewhere in the middle of her chest. Harry hadn't claimed the money. But she hadn't been totally wrong, because some other rightful owner hadn't claimed it, either.

She was right back where she had started with Harry, and that was a good thing because...because she had been enjoying her self-imposed task and wasn't quite ready to give it up. Yet.

"Interesting," Steph went on, "but it begs a couple of questions. One, why *was* Harry fibbing on the phone to you?"

Leave it to Little Miss Murder, She Wrote to narrow the focus to clues instead of basking in the happiness of what had—and hadn't—happened.

"I think," Acey declared, "that if I knew I possessed the only winning ticket and I heard that some other dude had come forward saying it was his, I might be a little too preoccupied to talk to some nosy chick like myself."

"All right," Steph allowed. "Point taken. Which leads us to the more important question. I saw what you went through today. Can you go through this agony a second time, when Harry really *does* come forward?"

Acey picked some stray cat hair off the arm of the sofa. "I don't know what you're talking about."

"Deny, deny, deny," Steph said, "but you dig this guy. Even if you say you can't dig him because he's rich. The idea of never seeing him again just about wrecked you tonight. Maybe this is more than you can handle."

Acey bristled.

"I'm serious, Acey. After Charlie, and you swearing off rich men, maybe you don't need to be hanging around another rich man so much, especially when you have such strong feelings for him."

"I don't—"

Steph held up her hand. "Save it. I may be the younger sister but I'm no idiot. Don't try to fool me, and don't try to fool yourself."

Acey scratched at the loose threads on the sofa, and one caught on her thumbnail. "I'm assuming this speech means you won't help me with my plan anymore?"

"If you continue with it, I promise I'll support you and help you the same way I've been doing. I just want you to consider how you felt today before you *do* continue."

Harry's face floated into Acey's mind, his bright smile making her almost squint from the inside out. She thought about how hard he worked every day.

It's worth it, it's worth it, it's worth it. "I'm doing the right thing. Full speed ahead."

Steph nodded, but only after the briefest of hesitations, which Acey noticed and ignored.

Chapter Eight

Harry couldn't help thinking, sitting next to Acey on his front stoop, that he had spent more time with this woman in the past two weeks than he'd ever spent in months with any other woman. Including his mother, sisters, and every woman he'd ever slept with.

In fact, maybe it was because he'd spent so much time with Acey that they couldn't decide what to do today. They'd tossed out a few dull ideas, and were now just sitting in silence.

"I'm sorry," Acey finally said. "I thought it would be fun to just drop by and do something spontaneous. It's my day off and all. But this isn't exactly a spontaneous town."

Harry *had* been surprised when Acey'd buzzed him a little while ago. He'd been at his desk, alternating between working and feeling guilty over fibbing to her the day before on the phone. It was easy to just avoid talking about his wealthy upbringing because it really didn't come up. It wasn't quite as easy to just make something up. He'd been remembering how she'd told him about Charlie, and the difficult things she'd been through, and he felt extra bad about not telling this honest, forthright woman the truth.

It was for her own good, he'd eventually consoled himself. After all, he wouldn't be able to convince any woman that money is meaningless if she knew he could have access to piles of it whenever he wanted.

"Why were you going for spontaneous, anyway?"

Acey raised her eyebrows. "If spontaneity had reasons, it would cease to be spontaneity."

"I love when a simple conversation takes a sharp philosophical turn."

"Come on," Acey said. "I thought you could use the company after having such a bad day yesterday."

Now it was Harry's turn to raise his eyebrows. "I had a bad day yesterday?"

Acey started just slightly, like a sparrow spotting a cat in the far distance and becoming extra cautious. "Not bad day, I meant...busy day. Remember, I called after you took a break?"

"Yes."

"You sounded a little strange on the phone, to be honest."

"So did you."

Acey went on as if she hadn't heard. "So I deduced you had a hard day at work on your grant, maybe getting some bad *news* or something, making it a bad day overall."

"Everything's all right. Don't worry."

"Are you having a better day today?"

Acey wasn't the easiest person to follow sometimes. Her sentences tended to tumble from her lips prematurely, as if they hadn't yet fully formed in her brain.

"I am now," he answered, taking warm pleasure at her unselfconscious beam. "Listen, let's just take a stroll. I like just walkin' and talkin' with you. We don't have to do anything much, or spend money, to have fun."

"Um, yeah. Sure."

They stood, just as Pete, his next-door neighbor's son, came barreling up the walk, almost crashing into Harry. He steadied Pete. "Whoa, there. In a hurry?"

"I have homework."

Harry exchanged a look with Acey, who he guessed was thinking the same thing: This kid had to be in third grade, tops. No third grader he'd ever met—when Harry was in third grade himself and since then—ever ran home to get a start on homework. "Well, Pete, that's real admirable."

"It is," Acey affirmed. "I bet a kid like you is already hitting the books so he can get into a great college."

Pete stared at her as if she'd sprouted a second nose. "I can't play outside until my homework's done."

"That explains it," Harry said, as Acey had the grace to look embarrassed. "How are your grades, by the way?"

Pete's somewhat logical reply was, "School's almost over."

"Ah," Harry said.

"I might fail my math test next week."

"Not if you study," Harry pointed out.

"I'm, like, really bad at math."

"I'm, like, pretty good at math," Harry said, "so if you need help, tell your mother I said you could knock on my door and I'll give y'all a hand."

"Okay," Pete said, scuffing his toe repeatedly on the front step. He was adopting a noncommittal stare at the ground, but Harry could tell the kid was glad for the offer. "I can't wait till school's done."

"I bet," Harry said.

"Mom said I have to help her out a lot this summer. Doing chores and watching my sister and stuff." He made a kid face of displeasure that Harry was tempted to laugh at. "But I have my things to do."

"Like playing ball?" Acey asked.

Pete glanced at her again, his expression revealing a little more respect. "Yeah. And Dad and Suzy are taking me to Disney World. Mom's not going. She hates Suzy."

"I'm sure your Mom would love to go to Disney World with y'all," Harry said, "but she has to work."

"Yup," Pete said, beginning to jiggle his leg a bit in that impatient way children had of showing grown-ups that valuable time is being wasted.

"See ya, Pete," Harry said, by way of dismissal.

"Bye, Harry," Pete flung over his shoulder as he pushed through the door. "Bye, lady!" he tacked on.

"Bye," Acey called, but Pete was long gone. "Cute kid," she said to Harry. "He must dig you. Kids never talk to me. Maybe I'm not so good with them."

"Sure, you are," Harry said, grinning. "Pete knows me, that's all. It's easier when kids know you or are related to you."

"It sounds like his mom's having a hard time."

"Yeah, I've met Peggy a few times," Harry said. "Her

husband left her for that woman and Peggy's pretty bitter. She works two jobs just to make ends meet. It's hard with two kids when you're alone, even with her alimony and child support."

"I regret saying that stupid thing about college," Acey said. "That poor mom's gonna have enough trouble paying for college in ten years."

"I agree."

They began a slow saunter down the walk and onto the sidewalk, and drifted to the right. "What Pete needs," Acey said, her measured words matching their snail's pace, "is a benefactor."

"A benefactor?"

"A patron."

Harry laughed. "Sounds like something out of a Dickens novel. Is that kind of thing even done anymore?"

"Why wouldn't it be?" Acey asked. "As long as there are still rich people and not-so-rich people. Pete needs a benefactor. I mean, doesn't he strike you as a smart kid?"

"Undoubtedly."

"Then he needs someone with *money* to make things happen for him. Don't you think?"

Harry shook his head, but not as if to say no. More to shake away the relentless *don't you think?*

"He needs someone rich," Acey surged on, "to recognize his brilliant potential, and pay his way through college. Then Pete could become a world-famous scientist."

"I think—"

"And maybe cure *cancer.*"

"Hold it." Harry stopped walking for a moment and looked at her. Then he almost forgot what he was going to say. Her skin was flushed from excitement at her idea, and the pink ran from her forehead into her cheeks, past her collarbone, and down into the scoop neck of her light blue shirt. He wondered at what point on her body her skin would pale again, but realized that staring into Acey's cleavage might not be the best way to make his point. His point again? Oh, yeah. "*I* recognize his potential, Acey."

"Yes, that's exactly what I meant!"

"Huh?"

She stammered a bit, then recovered. "Go on. Sorry to interrupt."

"I said, I recognize his potential and so I did something about it. Offered to tutor him. Because with his brains, combined with academic help from the right places, Pete can earn himself a scholarship. To whatever college he wants, perhaps."

"Oh."

"You see, it's not who you know, it's what you know. Don't you think?" He couldn't resist that last part.

Acey kicked a pebble. "Whatever." Then she continued walking and picked up the pace. Harry jogged a few steps to catch up with her and Acey stopped again.

At this rate, they'd never even make it to the corner, Harry thought.

"I couldn't hear you," Acey said.

"When?"

"Just now. You usually clunk around." She looked at his feet. "What are those?"

Harry lifted one foot and nearly had to squint at the shiny newness of his sneakers. "You like 'em? I just got 'em. Time to be a New Yorker, leave my ol' Texas boots in the closet for a while."

"Those are really nice." She crouched down to inspect them, and her hair fell over one shoulder, exposing the back of her creamy neck. Harry tried not to groan in lust.

"Nice brand name, there," Acey said, straightening up. "I think those are the sneakers in the new commercials."

"Yeah?"

"Yeah, which means I bet they were not cheap."

Oops. The one luxury he'd allowed himself in months. Months of walking New York's hard sidewalks in his boots had given him blisters. He'd broken down and bought himself some snazzy sneakers, partially because of all the walking he'd done and planned to keep doing with her, and she had caught it. Talk about not exactly setting an example of cheap livin'. "I, uh, got 'em on sale."

"Where?"

"I don't remember." She looked unconvinced until he added, "I'm a guy. I hate shopping. How am I supposed to remember where I buy things?"

She seemed to accept this explanation and they resumed their stroll a third time, and this time actually managed a bit of distance. At least until they were right in front of Bread and Milk, when a loud crash and louder yelp caused Harry and Acey to exchange a look before darting into the open door.

The magazine rack was lying facedown in the middle of the floor, as were piles of magazines. A spinner that was full of greeting cards also lay on its side, spilled cards around it. One card, on top of the pile, blared "Congratulations!" in red sparkly letters, which lent the mess a tiny bit of ironic humor.

"Is anyone hurt?" Harry asked Rosalia, who stood surveying the situation with twisted lips of annoyance.

"No, thank you, Harry," Rosalia said. "That woman by accident tipped this over, but I think she is okay."

Harry looked back at the fallen racks and spied a woman in a black sweater that had seen better days, rocking back and forth, biting the nails on both hands. Before he could place her, he heard Acey mumble, "Cassandra."

"Her name is Cassandra?" Harry asked.

"No!" Acey said in a fierce whisper. "That's just a nickname for her. She's been here for years, dispensing doom."

Ah, now Harry recognized the woman, who'd warned him once about the end drawing near. Which was probably true in the very long run, Harry thought, but she likely wasn't given any credit for her predictions.

Cassandra pointed a sharp, shaky finger at the magazines, which Acey was already beginning to gather neatly. "Do you see? Chaos! Like the chaos all around us!" She shuffled out of the store.

Acey threw up her hands and continued stacking magazines. Harry crouched down to help her.

"Ah," Rosalia said in disgust when she was gone. "Some people will make you *loco* as they are. Leave it, Acey, Harry. This is a good excuse. I didn't like the magazines anyway, the way they were set up. I'll think of something better."

Acey placed her hands on her hips, and Harry noticed the movement caused her T-shirt to tighten across her breasts. "Hmm," she said. "Can I offer a suggestion?"

"Please," Rosalia said, shoving a magazine away from her with one toe. "Can it get worse than this?"

"I guess not," Acey said. "Why don't you move the

entire magazine rack to the front of the store, instead of on the side wall here? That way, people can pick them up at checkout, like at a supermarket."

"I thought about that when I opened the store, but I thought, there are usually not long lines here. People just pick up one or two things they need."

Harry turned over an empty crate and sat.

"I still think it will work," Acey insisted, "because where you have it now, only the people who come in here with the intent to buy a magazine will find them. An impulse buy is more likely near the register. And, you can take these," she added, bending down to pick up some coloring books, "and comic books, and put them on the two bottom shelves. That way, they're at eye level with kids, who'll see them and want to buy them."

"That is a good idea."

"And you know what?" Acey continued, gathering steam. "You can take the greeting cards, and put them where the magazines were, so you have more room to spread them out. Then you should hang a nice calendar near the cards, with big holidays circled, and people will think about holidays when they see it, and be more likely to grab a card so they don't forget. And the little gift thingies at the counter now? You could move them back here with the cards, or…"

Sharp pain stabbed Harry's foot, and he realized that, as he was mesmerized by Acey, it had fallen asleep. He eased it out from underneath him, and though it prickled, he continued to watch Acey. If she was doing nothing but standing around, she would be beautiful on looks alone, but now, she was luminous. Her mind was running hard, her excited ideas pouring out as her cheeks flushed. Her hair fell into her face and she brushed it away not self-consciously but in an impatient shove so it wouldn't interrupt her flow.

"Harry, she is smart, no?" Rosalia suddenly said. Harry looked at the half smile on the older woman's face and realized he'd been caught. "Very," he replied. Rosalia nodded in satisfaction.

"And you have some nice fresh flowers in here," Acey said, ignoring the exchange. "At about five in the afternoon, you could put them in a bucket right outside the door—where you can keep an eye on them, of course—and people commuting back here from Manhattan can buy them, especially men, instead of buying them in the city and having them wilt in the train—"

"Wait," Rosalia cried. "I need to get a pen! I don't want to forget any of your good ideas."

Acey grinned, showing all her perfect teeth, and as she launched into an idea for a weekly customer contest, Harry had an idea of his own. He didn't know if he would call it good, but he knew if he didn't act on it soon, he could very possibly stop breathing.

Rosalia squinted down at her extensive list and looked up. "I can't read this. I need to put the bright lights on. The storm's coming, it's getting so dark."

As if in agreement, thunder rumbled down.

Harry had cleared the floor and righted the heavy magazine rack while the women brainstormed, and he now stood up from the crate he'd been resting on. "We'd better go."

"You should stay," Rosalia said, flicking on the lights. The fluorescence glared off the plastic-covered loaves of Wonder bread. "You'll get soaking wet."

"Don't worry, we won't," Acey said. "We'll run. We've been loitering here long enough anyway."

"You are both so helpful." Rosalia beamed. "Together, you are a good team."

Acey fell silent, apparently fielding this one to Harry. Harry cleared his throat and came up with, "Thanks."

"No, thank you," Rosalia answered. "Now run."

Acey called goodbye as she stepped outside, and Harry closed the usually open door behind them. A fat raindrop landed on his nose, then one poured down his ear, and when he turned his face accusatorily to the sky, one dropped into his eye.

"Let's see how good those new sneakers of yours are," Acey said, and took off.

Harry had gotten pretty accustomed to women squealing over his athletic prowess, and the fact that there wasn't an extreme sport he hadn't taken up and attempted to master. But that was before what happened, before he'd ruined his knee. He hadn't tested it at a pace faster than a quick walk before today. Luckily, Acey stayed in front, so she couldn't see him limping along. Also luckily, Acey was not very fast, so he didn't fall that far behind, even when it began to rain in sheets.

He half expected her to keep on running when they passed his building, to call a goodbye and head to her own apartment, but she streaked up his walkway and landed in his doorway. He crushed in, nearly on top of her.

"Not that I can get any wetter," Acey said, "but my shoes are beginning to slosh. I think I need to empty them out before I can keep going."

"This can't last long. Y'all can wait it out here. I just have to dig out my key." Harry tried to jam his hand into his jeans pocket, but it was sealed nearly shut from his drenching.

"Just like I waited out the storm that day at your place. Remember?"

Harry stopped trying to work his fingers into his pocket and looked at Acey. It was a blurrier view of her than normal, due to the fact that they were squashed together. She was heaving deep breaths from their dash, and he could feel every rise and fall of her chest against his forearm. Wind gusted at them, which should have made Harry shiver, but it didn't. He was hot.

He made one last valiant effort to fight himself.

"That was some impressive sprinting," he said, trying to laugh.

His eyes were on her lips when she replied, "Hey, this is New York. Don't you know? We move fast here." But she didn't carry off the confidence a line like that deserved. Her voice was shaking. Maybe *she* was shivering.

Or maybe…

"I had this idea," Harry confessed in a murmur.

Before confusion could spark in Acey's eyes, Harry reached out with both hands, and used both thumbs to ease her eyelids shut, brushing away the wetness in her lashes. Her lids trembled but stayed closed. He slipped his hands to either side of her head and moved his face until it was an inch from hers. He breathed in her sweet skin, and the scent of summer rain warming on her face.

He remained motionless, and he didn't know how long it was before her lips parted, before she rose up onto her toes and blindly but effortlessly covered his mouth with hers.

The sensitive skin of his lips dragged against hers

tentatively, barely moving, and Harry's heart and groin began to throb in synchronicity. The pressure increased, their lips flexing, hardening and softening. They were, at the same time, both initiating and following. Both slid their mouths open, both tongues darted then lingered, then pressed and swirled.

Acey's fingers grabbed at his hips, the waist of his pants, and tugged at his shirt hem. The touch of her fingertips against his bare skin made him start. She caressed and deepened the kiss even more. She clutched, those impressive nails digging in deep as she ground her hips into his upper thighs.

Harry moaned and pulled his fingers through her hair, grabbing it in heavy, soaking-wet fistfuls and squeezing until rainwater ran down his wrists and arms.

Neither pulled away until the air began running ragged through their nostrils and their bodies begged for more oxygen. They broke apart in a sudden mutual gasp.

Their mouths still open, they gaped at each other for a half second.

"I shouldn't have done that," they apologized simultaneously, and then both backed up a step, regarded the other and said, again simultaneously, "*You* shouldn't have done that?"

Silence.

Harry struggled for words, but the ever-verbal Acey was first.

"See ya," she said, and without even a meaningful look, bolted out of the doorway.

Harry watched her run down the street, flying even faster than before despite the aforementioned sloshy shoes, and despite the fact that the downpour had tapered off into a drizzle.

Chapter Nine

When Acey got home, she shed her wet clothing and flung it over the shower curtain bar to drip-dry. Wearing only a fresh bra and panties, she wrapped herself up in a zebra-print throw and padded in socks into the living room, where she curled up on the end of the sofa.

She stared at nothing, listened to nothing, but unfortunately her mind managed to keep itself occupied by rewinding and replaying, over and over, the tape of Harry kissing her.

Of her kissing Harry.

How could she have done that?

Their easy friendship had changed. Okay, so maybe it hadn't been a completely easy friendship. Acey allowed the relationship had been a bit tight with sexual tension all along. Still, she should have been able to fend that off. She'd had a job to do: Get Harry Wells to claim his millions. Instead, he'd taken the first step to laying claim on her heart. And she had let him.

She glanced around for something to distract her. If only she could sit down with a pint of ice cream and eat the whole thing in an emotional fit. But she was Italian. Italians savored and cherished the act of eating, and it would never do to just blindly choke down mouthfuls of anything. Besides, the idea of consuming an entire pint of ice cream was nauseating.

Still, maybe something cold wasn't a bad idea, Acey thought as, in her mind's eye, Harry once again twisted his fingers in her hair and pressed his hardness against her body. A cold shower?

Steph blew through the door with the after-storm wind. Acey, in her reverie, hadn't heard her approaching and felt somewhat disappointed. Much as she loved her sister, she needed to be alone to purge the memories from her brain so she could use the same brain to decide her next move.

Because she wasn't quitting now.

Although maybe she'd take a little break.

"Got caught in the rain again?" Steph asked, eyeing the towel turban on Acey's head. Acey nodded.

"Where did you go?"

"Just out for some exercise," Acey lied. "I stopped in Bread and Milk."

"Were we out of something?"

"No, Rosalia just needed a little help on a few things, and I, uh, volunteered."

"Oh," Steph said, and left it at that as she sailed into the next room. She emerged a few moments later in pink pajama bottoms and a tank top. Acey was surprised

Steph, aka Colonel Mustard, hadn't zeroed right in on her fairly obvious lie of omission, but when Steph plopped down beside her, Acey quickly found out why.

"I met someone. He asked me out. I said yes. Going out Friday, thank you very much." Steph ended in a singsongy voice.

Acey tried to muster a modicum of enthusiasm. "How great. I'm really happy for you. He's cute?"

"He's cute, and even cuter with the haircut he got with us today. He's a cop in Brooklyn."

Acey did laugh then. "A cop. How perfect for you."

"I know. I figure, if it doesn't work out, I can stay friends with him and use him…I mean, ask him politely to help me with research for my books."

"You're lucky."

"Yup." Steph pulled a throw pillow out from behind her back and flung it across the room. "Why isn't the TV on?"

"Why does it have to be?"

Steph made a face that reminded Acey of the instigating face she used to make, when they were kids, in the backseat of Dad's car. "What's *your* problem?"

Sherlock leaped with grace onto Acey's lap and she reached out to pat him, but he recoiled at the sight of the towel sticking like a growth out of the top of her head and moved to Steph's lap instead. Insulted by both roommates, Acey stood up. "I don't *have* a problem."

"You sound like it. Listen, if the phone rings, let me get it because it could be Fletch."

"The cop's name is *Fletch?* Are you for real? Is *he?*"

"It's Tom Fletcher but his friends call him Fletch," Steph said defensively.

"Oh, for crying out loud."

"Just shut up. What's the big deal what his name is? You're a pain today. Maybe if you weren't walking around all sexually frustrated every minute because of Mr. Moneybags—"

An indignant cry flew from Acey's throat.

"—you'd be a little nicer to me."

Acey leaped off the couch, her blanket falling to the floor in a heap at her feet. "Maybe I'd be a little nicer to you if you did something to deserve it."

"Like what? Get you a subscription to *Playgirl*?"

Acey picked up the pillow Steph had tossed on the floor and threw it hard at her. Steph ducked and it knocked a picture crooked on the wall. Sherlock fled for cover in the next room. "For your *information*..."

"Yeah?" Steph challenged, jumping to her feet.

"I... I..."

"'I... I...'" Steph mimicked. "Spit it out."

"I'm not going to see Harry for a while." Acey sat back down on the sofa again, avoiding eye contact with her sister. "Because, well, just because. *There,*" she added childishly. "If I can do that, it means I can't be all hot for him like you're accusing. So leave me alone."

Steph dropped onto the floor, apparently also out of steam. "What happened?"

"Nothing happened. Nothing important," Acey amended, ignoring her protesting heart.

They sat in silence for a few minutes.

"I'm sorry I jumped all over you," Steph finally said. "I just wanted you to be happy for me, and you sounded mopey instead and I acted like a big baby about it."

"No, I'm sorry," Acey countered. "You deserve to have a nice thing happen and I was being a nasty, selfish brat. I really am happy."

"Thanks." Steph curled her feet underneath her, leaned forward and dropped her chin in her hands, elbows on the floor. "I am really happy to have a date with a guy who actually sounds nice. It's been so long, you know? Ages. I was getting lonely."

"You were? How come you never said anything?"

"I figured it couldn't last forever. Plus, sometimes you don't tell your sister *everything*." She squeezed Acey's middle toe.

Acey thought about what she was keeping to herself.

Steph reached behind her, grabbed Acey's blanket and draped it over her older sister. "And I'm especially sorry about that crap I was saying about Harry. Maybe I was just jealous all along that you were seeing someone and…"

"I'm not… I wasn't *seeing* him."

"Well, you're not seeing anyone else. And I got a look at him out the window that day you went to the zoo. He's hunky."

Acey giggled at the juvenile word. "Hunky Harry."

"I'd be sexually frustrated if I was hanging around Hunky Harry. What's this about not seeing him anymore?"

Acey opened her mouth, then closed it again. *Acey never follows through.* Here she goes again, folks. Aborting another mission.

No, she told herself. No.

"No," she said out loud. "I wasn't serious about that. I'm just going to give it a couple of days' rest. I admit I find him somewhat attractive." She winced at her own understatement. "But you know what? That must be the money talking. I mean, what woman wouldn't be attracted to a multimillionaire?"

"You. I'm sorry to have to be the one to break it to you, but it looks as if you like Harry for *Harry.*" Steph held up a hand. "No, no need to tell me how brilliant I am. I already know."

"Smarty-pants."

"Smarty-*panties.* How 'bout putting some clothes on? You're offending me." Steph laughed, completely unoffended. "And you're sitting on the remote."

Acey felt underneath her, slid the remote out from between cushions and turned on the ever-faithful companion before heading to the bedroom. She caught her reflection in the mirror and stilled, quietly examining herself.

She wasn't one for excessive vanity. She fixed herself up in the morning and that was pretty much it for mirrors until she brushed her teeth at night. Now, though, as she looked at herself, she wanted to see whatever it was that Harry had seen, whatever it was that would have driven him to participate in that movie-scene makeout.

She dragged the towel off her head and scrunched strands of her hair. Then she closed her eyes, trying to feel Harry's hands and lips again. It was not difficult.

She sighed and fell onto her bed, a satisfying action even without a witness to its drama. She didn't have another day off until Saturday anyway, so she just would refrain from even speaking to Harry on the phone until then. That was three and a half days away. That should be plenty of buffer zone—enough time away from the kiss so she could act like nothing out of the ordinary had occurred.

She shook her head, back and forth, attention on the

ceiling. No way. Three and a half *years* wouldn't be long enough to wipe this memory away.

Dammit.

"Acey, come on," Steph said from the window.

"We're not playing with a time limit," Acey said, studying her little row of Scrabble tiles. There was no point in playing the game with Steph, who knew every word in the English language—and a few in other languages—and could beat world geniuses. Acey was no threat to Steph's sovereignty. However, Scrabble wasted time, which Acey was using too much of to remember a kiss. The kiss. She just had to stop. So she'd suggested a game.

Steph had gotten up to stare out the window while thickheaded Acey struggled to make a word. Finally, Acey extracted two tiles and laid them on the board. "There."

Steph glanced over from where she stood. *"Cow?"* she asked. "That's your word?"

"There's nothing else," Acey said. "My tiles are crap."

"Let me see," Steph said, turning her sister's rack around. Acey let her. They'd played like this for years. Steph picked up three more tiles. "Just for the sake of more points," she explained as she turned *Cow* into *Cowboy*.

Acey glared at her. Steph laughed as the buzzer sounded. "Wonder who that is. Can you go?" Steph asked. "I have to go to the bathroom and the buzzer's broken on our end."

"Since when?" Acey asked. Steph shrugged and trotted off. Acey sighed and clattered down to the front door.

Harry stood there, with a pile of papers in his arms. The sky behind him was changing, displaying an iridescent orange glow of a sunset, but Harry was the focus of the picture. Shadows played over his shoulders and light sifted golden through his hair.

"Hi," Acey managed. "I was, um, going to, well. Hi."

Kissing. Pressing, moaning, squeezing, grabbing…

"Is this a bad time? I know it's your day off, but I don't want to interrupt anything important."

Tasting, grasping, nibbling. Acey couldn't think properly. "Was there something you wanted?" she asked, and chastised herself for her unfortunate phrasing.

Harry couldn't tell this woman what he wanted for two reasons: One, she might boot him off her stoop and refuse to speak to him for the rest of her life or, two, she might jump on him, wrap her legs around his waist and invite him in for a night of passionate lovemaking that would ruin his opportunity for doing the right thing by a good woman.

He wasn't willing to risk either one, so he decided to stick with the actual reason he'd dropped by.

"I was messing around on the Internet," he said, and she looked confused, so he hurried his explanation along. "I found some things I thought you might want to take a look at, or work on." He handed her the stack of papers.

She reached out and glanced at the top one. It was upside down, so she twisted her neck a bit to read it. Her eyebrows pushed together as she flipped through the papers underneath. "Are these college applications?"

"No, not exactly. They're applications for grants. For, well, yeah, for college."

"This is one of the nicest things anyone has ever done for me, because you have faith in me."

"It never occurred to me not to have faith in you."

"I'm going to study these applications," Acey said. "I promise."

"Don't promise me. I'm not insulted no matter what you do. It's all your choice. I just made some friendly suggestions."

"If I go for this, I will need help. I'll call you."

"I hope you do call," he said, and in the interest of regaining a modicum of control, added, "even if you don't need help."

He longed to touch her. For a moment, he actually willed a lock of her hair to fall across her forehead so he could have an excuse to brush it away for her, his fingertips once again grazing the skin that he had clutched so desperately only a few days ago. But, he knew, he had no right to it, and no right to even wish it. He'd already trespassed over his strict parameters with Acey Corelli. Time to put up his invisible electric fence.

Especially since it appeared Acey had constructed her own.

"Bye," he said, and his hand twitched so he held it up in a weak wave. Acey, both hands full, chose to nod her chin at him once.

He turned to go, and was stopped by a request to wait.

Harry pivoted.

"Thank you," she said simply.

Harry liked the smile that went with the thank-you. It wasn't a wide grin. In fact, it was rather tiny, but it looked as if she couldn't help it, that it was a small indulgence she was allowing herself.

It was better than the words.

"You're welcome," he said. "Bye, now."

Before he was even out of her sight, Acey wanted to implore him back but she was too strong, and she cursed that strength—colorfully—as she made her way back to her apartment.

"The buzzer's not broken," Steph said as Acey passed her. "I saw him out the window."

Acey didn't answer. She went to their room and dropped the applications on the bed. The papers broke from the pile and fanned out across the bedspread, and Acey stared at them.

How had this gotten so out of hand? How had she gone from trying to tie up Harry's future with a ribbon to Harry handing her back her own future in brightly colored paper?

Name, read the top line on one page, and farther down, *Social Security Number,* and a bit farther down, *Desired Course of Study.* Acey felt a tiny thrill even though up until very recently, she had no knowledge of desiring anything until it showed up at her doorstep.

Until *all* of it showed up at her doorstep.

It occurred to Acey that Harry was in a position to just offer to give her tuition if that's what he really wanted to do. Not that she would ever have accepted it, but most likely, that was why he hadn't offered. Well, that and the small fact that he still had not claimed his cash. But something about giving her the applications, and implying she could get this done on her *own* merit, without charity—that, she could accept.

Acey walked to work the next day to the echo of the church bells dismissing the last early-afternoon Catholic

Mass. She tried to just listen to the beautiful chimes, but her thoughts, and her guilt, insisted on breaking through.

She told herself that losing the guilt of making Harry's acquaintance under false pretenses would smoothly pave the way for her Make Harry Rich plan to continue, but if she was honest with herself, she would have to admit that she'd also like to pave the way for him to help her with these applications.

Acey had had a dream last night. She was sitting in a college classroom and was called on to solve a nearly impossible equation. She'd approached the blackboard with uncharacteristic confidence, and heard the sharp collective intake of breath when she'd rapidly filled the double chalkboard with symbols and number combinations that she couldn't fathom in her waking state. When she finished, she turned around in triumph, but everyone—her classmates and her professor—had disappeared. The only person remaining was Harry Wells, sitting in the back right corner, and he was clapping his hands slowly, speeding up when she took a bow just for him. When she'd raised her head again, she was awake in her bed, seeing nothing but shadows on her ceiling and hearing nothing but Steph snoring in the next bed.

Acey faced her truth—she wanted Harry to help her with her applications. She wanted to see if she could change her future.

Oh, hell—she wanted Harry.

Which would make working with him on these applications impossible, right? Cooperation from Harry meant proximity. And Acey knew that these days, being adjacent to Harry put her in physical pain. That kind of physical pain where you haven't eaten in twenty-four hours, and someone right next to you is enjoying a hot meatball hero. Well, maybe that wasn't quite right, but food analogies always came easiest for Acey.

It was in this frame of mind that Acey pushed the door open to Focaccia's and was faced with a relationship-and-food situation. The only really surprising thing about it was that it had nothing to do with either Lydia or Anthony.

A girl in strange blond dreadlocks was shouting to the air behind the counter. An upset Lydia and a bewildered Anthony were standing close together in a corner, observing. Good thing it was still fifteen minutes to their Sunday noon opening, or customers would have been scampering out of the way of the thick tension.

Lydia gestured for Acey to come over to her, and Acey obeyed.

"What the heck's this all about?" Acey asked.

"Steve!" the girl bellowed. "Get out here and face me! Back away from betrayal!"

"Steve?" Acey asked incredulously. "That's Steve's girlfriend?"

"When I got here," Lydia said in a stage whisper, "she was waiting. She said she was Steve's girlfriend, said her name's Milla. So what was I gonna do? Leave her on the street? I let her in."

"A betrayal of the body is a betrayal of the soul!" Milla screamed, pounding one fist on the counter. Acey, Lydia and Anthony all flinched.

"Well, Steve shows up here," Lydia continued, "and takes one look at Milla and suddenly she's World War Three."

"Sounds like they had some kind of fight last night," Anthony contributed, "and Steve must have walked out on her, so she shows up here today to keep it going."

"She's freaking out and yelling," Lydia cut in, "and Steve—you know Steve, he never says a bad word to anyone—just silently walks into the back pantry and closes the door."

"The thing is," Anthony added, "he grabbed one thing to take with him into that closet."

Acey's heart plummeted. "Oh, my God, not…not…" A knife? Steve?

"No," Lydia said. "A humongous Italian sausage."

"Don't do this, Steve!" Milla screamed. "You don't want to do this! You just want to spite me!"

Ah, Acey thought. A little evil revenge on the vegan girlfriend. The corners of her lips twitched in appreciation. Who knew Steve had it in him?

"Uh, we open in ten minutes," Acey pointed out.

"I tried to make Milla calm down and leave," Lydia said. "She went into this weird trance thing. Closed her eyes and chanted in another language and breathed in and out really hard for about a minute. Then she just started freaking out again."

"She's not going anywhere anytime soon," Anthony said.

"Steve!" Milla bellowed. "I want to *talk* to you!"

"At least she's staying on that side of the counter," Lydia said. "I warned her if she didn't, I'd call my dad. And the cops. Which I might very well end up doing anyway."

Acey ducked under the counter and knocked on the pantry door. "Steve? It's Acey. Come on, open up."

The door opened one little crack. "Acey?"

She tried to pull the door open, but Steve was holding tight to the knob on the other side. "Are you really eating that sausage?"

"Right now I'm just smelling it," Steve confessed. "But I *will* eat it if she doesn't leave."

"I hate to say it, but she is right that you shouldn't do it to spite her."

"No, I'll be doing it because I *like* sausage. I gave it up for her."

"I know." Acey sighed.

"Make her go away."

"I'm trying to think of something. We're all on your side."

Anthony joined Acey at the closet. "Yo, Steve, hang in there, buddy. Don't do anything I wouldn't do."

"Meaning what?" Steve asked.

"I dunno."

"Anthony," Acey pleaded, clutching at the front of his T-shirt. "Can't you do something?"

"No way," Anthony said. "Listen, if that was a half-a-dozen goons with baseball bats ready to mess Steve up for a gambling debt, I could handle that. A girl-friend, no. Not my department."

Whose department would it be? Acey wondered, watching the minute hand inch toward the twelve.

Someone who could charm any woman he came across.

"Stay with Steve," Acey ordered Anthony, and ran to the phone. She dialed the number she shamefully knew by heart.

"Hello?"

"Harry," Acey cried. "I need you."

She heard him choke on his own breath, and she quickly clarified. "I mean, I need your help. Please? It won't take long."

"Anything. Are y'all at home? Are you okay?"

"I'm fine, it's not me. I'm at Focaccia's. There's a situation here that needs, uh, defusing. Some diplomatic Southern charm. Can you come here right now?"

"I'm on my way."

"Thanks, and Harry?" she tacked on before he hung up.

"Yes?"

"Wear your cowboy boots."

There was a funny little silence, and Harry uncertainly answered, "Okay," before she heard the click.

"Steve!" Milla wailed.

Acey walked over to where the distraught girl stood. She felt a little sorry for Milla, standing there in her colorless hemp shirt and ragged jeans. "Milla, look. I understand you want to talk to Steve but we're opening in a couple of minutes and you're going to upset the customers."

"The customers should *thank* me," Milla practically spit. "You're selling them toxic poison for their bodies."

The nasty comment sideswiped Acey. Wasn't the whole vegan/vegetarian thing generally done out of love and peace? She decided to attribute Milla's vitriol to young love and brokenheartedness.

Others weren't so ready with forgiveness. "I will kill that woman," Acey heard Lydia say. She turned to find Anthony restraining his girlfriend by her elbows. "That's my family's business you're slamming!" Lydia yelled.

"Then your family's business can take responsibility for the ill health of this entire community!" Milla snapped back.

"I'll be responsible for ill health, all right! *Yours!*" Lydia roared.

The door swung open and a smooth, patient drawl stopped everyone cold.

"What seems to be the trouble, ladies?"

Acey was grateful she'd forgotten to lock the door behind her earlier. Harry stepped into the room, his boots producing a *clunk-clunk* in the suddenly quiet room. Milla turned to face him and they regarded each other. Acey glanced at the clock. High noon. She half expected to hear a horse whinnying outside. She reminded herself that if she did, it would be because someone had left the door open at the off-track betting up the street, and not because Harry Wells had morphed into John Wayne.

She was extra glad for those boots. She'd requested them because they seemed like the finishing touch for a man no woman could resist. They made him look like a hero.

Her hero.

Or not, she reprimanded her beating heart and pounding blood.

"Who are you?" Milla stammered. Yes, stammered, proving Acey's hypothesis: Harry affected every woman the same way.

"Who are you?" was Harry's comeback.

"My boyfriend is…he's locked in the closet…"

"I see," Harry said, but Acey didn't know how he could.

"…with a big sausage," Milla finished weakly.

"Her boyfriend is…?" Harry asked Acey.

"Steve," she said. "You know, the young guy that works here? The vegan? That's Milla."

"Ah, well." Harry beckoned her over, and just as he did, the first customer of the day pushed through the door, followed by another, and another, until there was a line of people calling orders. Acey, Lydia and Anthony got right to work pushing pizza across the counter, but every few seconds, Acey would look up at Milla and Harry, who were now in a booth. The first couple of times she looked, Milla was tearfully explaining something to Harry, but then every time Acey glanced over after that, Harry was talking. She didn't know what he was saying, but his face was soft and calm, and Milla eventually stopped blowing her nose on napkins from the dispenser. Finally, without another outburst, she left Focaccia's.

Turning her head to either side to make sure Anthony couldn't overhear, Lydia muttered to Acey, "Don't get me wrong, I love my man." She stared at Harry. "But I'm so totally in love with this cowboy dude."

Acey went over to the pantry and rapped on the door. "Coast is clear, carnivore. Come on out."

Steve emerged, blinking at the overhead light. He still held the sausage, but it appeared unnibbled.

Anthony poked his head around the corner. "Hand over the meat," he said, grinning. "I'll make you a huge sausage hero with it and you can eat it slowly. My treat."

"Nah," Steve said. "I realized I didn't really want it after all. I did some thinking in there. The truth is, I feel pretty good lately, and it must be the diet. I'm going to try to keep it up."

"Good for you," Acey said.

"How'd you get her to go away?"

"We didn't," Acey said. "My, uh, friend over there did. He's good at helping people in distress."

"Women specifically, she means," Anthony said. "I don't see what's so great about him myself."

Acey considered drawing up a list but decided that could take up most of her shift.

Steve handed her the sausage and joined the others at the counter. Acey grimaced and dropped the meat discreetly into the trash. Then she peeled off her apron and sneaked out to the booth where Harry still sat.

"Hey," she said, sliding in. She was unprepared—though she shouldn't have been—for the triumphant grin he gave her. "Th-thank you."

"No problem. Sometimes it takes an outsider to fix things. Still, you'd better tell Steve to talk to that woman, whether he wants to patch things up or not. He's young, he'll learn how to handle a woman."

"Oh, *will* he now?"

"Yup, that kind of knowledge comes with age."

"I just bet." Acey would have challenged him but the sparkle in those eyes told her he was joking. The sparkle in those eyes… She cleared her throat.

"What I really mean," Harry added, "is that a real man faces situations head-on. He doesn't run away from confrontation."

Acey was not stupid, and so she recognized this as a nonsubtle reference to her disappearing act after their nonsubtle kiss. Especially with the way he was eyeing her now—yup, couldn't get any more obvious if he shone a beacon on it.

Kissing, licking, stroking…

Okay. She could have a discussion with him about it, where she would end up confessing she couldn't share space with him without gasping for air, or she could go for the ignore-it-and-hope-it-goes-away trick.

Hmm. Door number two, please. "You get a pie on the house for this one. Name your toppings."

Harry didn't even pretend to appear taken aback by her subject change. Possibly just used to it by now. "Any kind. Does my freebie include a delivery fee?"

"Huh?"

"I'm not hungry now because I ate a late breakfast, but I will be hungry. I anticipate wanting some pizza right around the end of your shift. So how about some door-to-door service?"

"You've got to be kidding."

"I even wore the boots," Harry pointed out. "Y'all didn't even tell me why. I ran all the way here, and it would have been much easier in my comfy new sneakers."

Acey gave in. As a daughter in an Italian-American family, guilt worked on her in strange ways. "Fine. But how about coming to my place instead?"

"Why?"

"Because...because then we can work on my applications." *With Steph's adult supervision. To keep us from doing anything stupid. Or hot. Or X-rated.*

"You've decided to try?"

"Well, since you went to the trouble and all."

"That's why? Because I went through the trouble?"

She stared at the table, then lifted her chin firmly to look him in the eye. "No. I'm doing it because I want to. Because I want to see if I can do it. If we can do it."

He winked at her, and for a long moment, it was like a movie where the hero winks in slow motion and the scene fades away.

Chapter Ten

Acey flipped the notebook around and pushed it toward Harry. He reached up from his spot on the carpet and slid the notebook off the bed above him, where Acey sat cross-legged.

For two people who were carefully and obviously trying to avoid sexual stimulation, the bedroom was probably the last place they should have been. But the computer was in there, and there was no getting around that situation unless they unhooked the entire setup and moved the equipment and power surger to the living room. Which, uncomfortable as they were, they might even have attempted, but the computer monitor was covered with trinkets and sticky notes with Web site addresses, and dismantling the whole thing didn't seem worth the certain wrath it would incur from Steph. Who, by the way, wasn't there to ask, having taken Sherlock to a late vet appointment that Acey swore she never knew about. The geometric screen saver danced while Acey and Harry worked.

"How does that grab you?" Acey asked now.

She waited patiently while Harry read her paragraph. He hid a smile. It was clear writing was not Acey's strong suit, judging by the fact that this small paragraph had taken almost forty-five minutes to write, and that half of it was scratched out. What remained, however, were not Acey's words. They were the words of someone making liberal use of a thesaurus.

"It reads fine," Harry began, "technically. But I'm not hearing your voice."

"What do you suggest?"

"The people who are offering the grant are just people, right?"

"Yeah."

"So show them *Acey*. Tell these people why you, Acey, deserve their generosity. Let you come through. The Acey I know and..."

He stopped and felt a weird, unfamiliar heat flare behind his ears. Was he blushing? He'd never done it before, so he was uncertain.

Acey laid down her pen. "Before we continue," she said, "I propose that we, as adults, acknowledge the gorilla in the room."

Harry reached up onto what he assumed was Steph's bed and pulled down a stuffed monkey. "This one?" He tossed it at Acey.

"Very funny. I mean the...thing that happened between us. It was...it was..."

"Yeah," Harry said. "It definitely was."

"Right. But we shouldn't have…we shouldn't have…"

"No. We definitely shouldn't have. I have my reasons, and you have…your reasons?"

"Yes. Reasons. But we're grown-ups, and we are capable of working together. Actually, you know what?" She held up the gorilla. "This is the gorilla in the room. It's going to sit on the edge of the bed here, between us. Anytime we feel the need to acknowledge it, we just pat him on the head." She demonstrated.

Harry did the same, feeling ridiculous.

"Very good. Now, you were saying?" She scrunched her nose. "Right, making the essay sound like me. I'm afraid if I do that, they'll see through me."

"What do you mean?"

"If I submit it like it is now, if I make myself sound smart, then they have a reason to throw money at me. If I sound like me, they won't be fooled. They'll see right through it, and know I'm trying to cash in on my shiny personality because my brain is nothing special."

"If I didn't see special smarts, would I have gone through all this trouble for you?" Harry shot at her.

"I guess not."

Harry pointed at her pen. "Write it again, but as if you're talking to friends. Be honest. Be you, which no other applicant can be." *Believe me,* he silently added. *No one.*

She appeared unconvinced but bent her head over the notebook again.

This time, she wrote and scratched for over an hour. Harry watched her flip her hair out of her face, then stop writing to gather it into a sloppy ponytail before continuing. He watched the tightness of her fist as she scratched, and the loosening of her fingers as she wrote in her loopy script. In between sentences, when she paused to consider, her toes wiggled inside their white socks.

When she was done, Harry discovered he'd been furiously rubbing the top of the gorilla's head, and suspected he had been for some time.

If Acey noticed, she was discreet. Instead she said, "This feels personal."

Harry yanked his hand away, and she clarified, "The essay."

He forced himself to concentrate again. "Good. It should."

"Before you read it, you have to share something personal, too."

Harry's guard went up. "Like what?"

"Like anything. Between this essay and you knowing my whole ex-boyfriend saga, you have a much bigger storage of info on me than I do on you."

"So? Is this a contest?"

"No. This is a friendship," Acey said firmly. "Spill."

"Gee, no pressure or anything." She didn't respond, just watched his face, disconcerting him even further. He thought that even if there weren't a whole bunch of things he'd rather she didn't learn, even if he had his whole history to honestly pick and choose from, he wouldn't know what she needed to hear at this very moment.

After a minute of silence, Acey asked, "How about your family?"

"I told you everything worth telling in that department," he assured her. Too fast? He slowed down. "Mother, father, sisters. Texas."

"Some kind of falling-out with your family?"

"Why do you ask?"

"You don't say anything about them, ever."

"We're not having a falling-out, exactly. I just decided recently that I needed to live in a certain way, outside their sphere of influence. They, well, let's just say that I know what's best for me at this point. And as much as they care about me, they don't know what's best for me. The thing is, they're very persuasive. So I try to keep my distance."

"I don't mean to offend you, but aren't you kind of old for this kind of predicament? Most people have the living-their-own-lives power struggle with their parents when they're about to enter college."

He grimaced. "You're right. I bet y'all think that at my advanced age, I should be having the arguments about what's best for me with a wife instead."

Acey laughed out loud, and hard. She wiped one eye with the back of her hand and asked, "That's your opinion of marriage, cowboy?"

"Not all marriages. I was kidding around. My parents have a good marriage, for the most part."

"Mine, too." She took a few post-laugh breaths. "Do you—did you leave someone special behind in Texas?"

"I left a lot of special someones behind," Harry answered. "As well as quite a few not-so-special someones. But that was all before I actually left Texas. There's no unfinished business there." He softened his tone at the end of the statement, in case Acey was searching for reassurance.

She nodded once, as if to say that was that. Then she moved on with the interview. "What are you afraid of?"

"What makes you think I'm afraid of anything?"

"Everyone's afraid of something, Harry."

"Oh, y'all meant in general. I thought you were asking what I'm afraid of right this minute."

"Could be."

Harry looked away. A small wind blew through her open window, ruffling the diaphanous, peach-colored curtains. It was a pretty sight, but on closer inspection, Harry could see loose threads along the bottom of the raggedly cut material. He tried to begin the sentence with "I'm afraid," but he couldn't. Acey would just have to understand that part. "Of losing myself," he said. "Of having recently understood myself and what was underneath years of mistakes and stupidity, and of maybe having that understanding only a short time before I lose it again. Because I always make another stupid mistake."

Harry hoped Acey's long silence was to assure that he was finished answering, rather than abject horror at his confessional. He was about to ask her when she spoke.

"I don't have a clue what you were like before I met you," she said. "All I know is that if you're afraid of not being the man you are now, that's crazy. Just wrong. The man you are now is effortless."

Harry turned his head to stare at Acey. She colored pinkish but kept talking.

"You help every single person you come across. You do a job designed to help those in need. You don't wait to be asked, you're just somehow always standing there with the right gesture or the right word. Particularly for me. So..." Her confident voice tapered off, as if she were aware she was treading in a minefield. "I have no idea what could happen that would cause a man like you to change. Don't let an opportunity pass you by because you are afraid of changing. Fate won't change you. You'll change *it* instead."

Harry was floored, even though that was already technically where he was sitting. Every word Acey had used described the man he'd so desperately wanted to be when he left Texas. Now, she was confirming he had done it.

Another thing: She'd said, *Don't let an opportunity pass you by,* and it sounded as if she had a specific opportunity in mind. Wait. Wayne. Of course. Wayne had said that to him, also. Don't let an opportunity pass you by. He had been talking about Acey. Was Acey talking about Acey? Was she having a change of heart about her reasons? About their kiss?

Was he?

He reached his hand up, but where he thought it would touch the synthetic fur of the stuffed gorilla, it touched smooth, soft flesh. The flesh of Acey's hand, which was already there, her fingers curling into the fluff. Harry didn't remove his hand, and Acey didn't move hers. Every nerve ending in his body came alive. He forced himself to look right into Acey's eyes and she did the same. Her eyes were wide, and her lips were moist, as if she'd just licked them in anticipation of something that had to come next.

And would have come next, if what actually came next hadn't.

The door to the apartment banged open, and a burst of loud, racking female sobs exploded into the already-charged silence. They were the kind of sobs that one held in tight, waiting until arriving home to fall under the overwhelming release.

"Steph?" Acey called, panic in her voice. She yanked

away from Harry, the gorilla, and the notebook and rushed out of the room. Out of discretion, Harry didn't follow. The sisters' privacy was their right in their own home.

He couldn't help it if Steph's agonized voice carried into the bedroom. "Acey, I can't believe this!" she wailed, her voice wet and gurgly. "What are we going to do?"

Harry heard Acey's soothing "shhs" and pictured her putting a protective arm around her younger sister. Steph's sobs dissolved into snuffles, and he heard her blow her nose. He got up then to close the door. Poor Steph probably had boyfriend problems, and she didn't need to find out he had heard everything. He was acting partly out of kindness, but also partly out of selfishness—he didn't want his first meeting with Acey's sibling to go badly.

When he got to the door, however, a word stopped him cold: tumor.

"A tumor. He has a tumor," Steph said.

"What?" Acey's voice was filled with disbelief. "How could that be? He looks perfectly healthy."

Harry remained frozen. Someone was dying?

"Well, he's *not* perfectly healthy," Steph said. "The vet said he has to have it removed."

Vet? Oh, Harry realized. The cat.

"It's my fault," Steph continued, fresh sobs erupting. "He was due last month for the checkup. I put it off because we didn't have the money, what with Mom's birthday and all."

"No. It's not your fault," Acey assured. "In fact, it's better. What if you had taken Sherlock a month ago and they'd found nothing, and then the tumor started growing the next day? We wouldn't have taken him in then until he got sick, and then it would have been way too late. No," Acey repeated, "nothing's your fault. It was caught early. It could be benign, right?"

Harry made a conscious effort to stop listening. He ordered himself to close the door. Difficult as it was to hear the women's suffering, this was their private business. But then he heard Acey exclaim, "How much?"

"A thousand dollars." Steph's voice was flat and resigned. "To take out the tumor and test it."

"Oh, my God," Acey said. "We don't have that kind of cash."

"I know, believe me."

"It's not even like we have it and we'll make do without other things for a while. We just have no savings. We don't have it."

"I know," Steph said, crying again.

"Mom and Dad would give it to us if they had it, but they don't. Who does? No one."

Then Harry's heart began to tear in two, because he heard Acey begin to cry also. "This is terrible," she said. "You love him so much. *I* love that little brat. Sherlock's our family. He trusts us to take care of him."

Steph apparently was crying too hard to answer, because the conversation ceased for a few minutes.

"We'll do something," Acey said, her hard words cutting through. "We'll explain to the landlord. He's not a jerk. Then maybe that will get us part of it."

"How are we gonna pay two rents next month?"

"We'll think about that then. We can both try to get some extra shifts."

"A thousand dollars' worth? Even if the salon and Focaccia's were open twenty-four-seven and we worked around the clock, we couldn't swing it."

"I said, we'll find a way," Acey said. "He just can't die." Her voice broke. "He can't die."

She can't die...she can't die...

Acey's words hurtled Harry back in time.

"...Harrison Wells, riding Belle of the Ball, owned by Lara Beck of Beck and Call Stables."

Harry and Belle strode into the ring. Belle, a large gray Dutch warmblood mare, tossed her head in the manner of her golden-haired owner. Harry turned his head to the stands, where Lara sat in her pink Chanel suit, waving a tiny ladylike wave. As always, she'd look stunning beside him, he in his crisp jacket and tall black boots.

Lara had wanted her beloved Belle to compete today here in Houston, aware that the pricey animal had been trained at an early age to jump her way to big prizes. Lara, however, doubted her own experience at this elite grand prix level, and had planned to skip the competition for one more year.

Then one night about a month prior, as Lara was shaking off the last orgasmic tremors, he offered to ride Belle in the grand prix. Lara was unconvinced at first. Harry did have more hubris, but technically even less experience than she did. Harry then pointed out that for years, in competitions just a step below, he'd consistently galloped rings around the other show jumpers. He was sure that her prize mare would be the one to carry him to victory. Lara finally relented and, since they were already in bed, Harry went about showing his gratitude.

Lara and Harry both knew their relationship wasn't serious, just a mutual appreciation of physical perfection. The horse arrangement was one of many benefits of their association.

Now, as Belle pranced into the arena, Harry smiled, causing his hunt cap's chin guard to tighten. They would jump this round clear, bump off any wannabes in the jump-off, and win. Then Harry would have the satisfaction of mastering another sporting challenge. Because that's what life was about when you had all the money and time in the world—testing how far the world could take you. Until then, he'd gone pretty far.

Next weekend was hang gliding, and the weekend after that would be…

The buzzer sounded, and Harry wrenched his concentration back to the task at hand. He collected Belle into a tight canter, counted strides to the first fence, and felt her able muscles bunch underneath him as they sailed easily up and over.

They took the oxer, the water jump, and the triple combination all in literal stride. Harry was already anticipating the final fence, which had complicated brush decorations that had caused four competing horses to spook.

The little fence before it was a gimme, just a small white thing, hardly a menace.

Maybe it was his mental dismissal that did it. Maybe Belle could sense her partner wasn't quite with her, felt alone when she galloped up to the small white fence. Maybe Harry would be wondering for the rest of his life.

Belle hesitated a fraction of a second, not enough to spot in the countless slow-motion cable TV replays later, but enough to alert Harry that her momentum had broken. She took the jump, and Harry was thrown unsteady in the saddle. As Belle landed, the weight on her back was distributed all wrong, jostling Harry's full weight onto her shoulders. Her strong legs weren't strong enough, buckling, and she went down.

Harry didn't have time to bail. He hit the ground nearly the same time Belle did, and his leg crunched as the distressed mare rolled on top of it. He tried to get away, crawl away, but his elbows just dug deep holes in the dirt. He resigned himself to bearing the pain until Belle pushed herself up, the reliable instinct of a horse who's fallen. But Belle didn't get up.

Harry tried to lift his head to see, but his helmet had been knocked askew and it pressed into one eyelid. Then a rushing black swept over his face and head, and he lay back down.

He didn't know if it was two minutes or two hours later when he heard, "Harry!" in his ear. Then an unrecognizable male voice said, "He's all right, a concussion, his leg's badly banged up, but he'll live. His poor horse ain't so lucky."

"Belle!" Lara cried, transferring her compassion from the man who'd brought her horse to this fate to the horse herself. "She can't die," she sobbed. "She can't die, she can't die."

Harry, in his black haze, felt Lara rocking back and forth beside him, at Belle's head. He knew, right then, Harrison Wells had died, too, leaving someone different behind, lying broken in the dry dust.

Without thinking, Harry left Acey's bedroom, hobbling only the tiniest bit on his reminder, and entered the living room.

Steph gasped. "You scared me! What did you do, come in through a window?"

"He's been here," Acey said quickly.

"He's been here the whole time?" She didn't sound embarrassed, just confused.

"We were busy."

Steph glanced from Acey to Harry and covered her mouth with her hand. "I'm sorry," she said through her fingers. "This really tops things off. I certainly didn't mean to interrupt."

"You didn't," Acey said.

Steph raised her brows over a pair of dark Acey-like eyes, but the physical similarities pretty much stopped there, Harry noticed. She was smaller than her older sister—her shoulders were bonier, her hips narrower, and her shorter brown hair even made her head look smaller. Her face was pierced in several places, and although Harry himself wasn't partial to it, he could easily see how she could bewitch other men. The jewelry made her appear exotic, as if she'd stepped out of some ancient tribe to try out life in Valley Stream for a while.

Acey clarified, "He was helping me do some, ah, paperwork."

"Paperwork for what?"

"It's not important," Harry said. "Or, it is important, but at the moment, it's not the priority. Are you all right? I tried not to listen," he apologized, "but it's a small apartment."

"No, that's all right," Steph said. "You just startled me. I'm Stephanie."

"I'm Harry," he said, shaking her cool hand.

Acey gave Harry a lame little shrug.

Harry smiled. "I would have forgotten about the man in the apartment, too, if my sister came in with bad news." He saw Sherlock lounging in Steph's lap, appearing not at all sick but happily snoozing, while Steph stroked him with trembling fingers.

"But I'm coming in with good news," Harry went on. "I'll give you the money."

Both sisters stared at him, mouths agape. Steph was the first to break the astonished silence. "You would do that for us?"

"Of course, he would," Acey said to Steph, "but he's not going to." She looked at Harry again. "That's… that's more than generous. Thank you, but we can't accept that."

"Why not?"

"Why not? Because it's one thousand damn dollars, that's why not."

"So I heard."

"How could you afford to give us—" Steph began, and then cut herself off, as if remembering something. "Oh," she said very quietly.

Harry lost the opportunity to ask her what she meant by that because Acey spoke up again. "You are very sweet, and very kind, but we *cannot* accept a handout like that from you."

"We could," Steph said, extremely reasonably, "perhaps accept a loan."

Acey turned and shot Steph a look that appeared to startle her little sister into shutting up. "May I talk to Harry alone for a minute, please?"

Steph nodded and rose, cradling Sherlock to her chest. Sherlock, not understanding that all the concern in the room was for his benefit, stretched his front paws out and rested his furry head on her shoulder contentedly.

"Sherlock will be fine," Acey assured. "He'll have

the operation. We'll find the money, don't worry. Lie down and try to relax. You had a rough time."

"Okay," Steph said. "You're right." She disappeared down the hall.

Acey stood and faced Harry. She had to incline her neck a bit to do so, as facing him head-on would have meant addressing his chest.

"Harry," she said. "I can't take a thousand dollars from you."

"Why not?"

Acey closed her eyes for a moment and prayed for the strength to turn down the help he was offering. "Remember at the zoo, I wouldn't even let you buy me a hot dog?"

"Yeah."

"If I wouldn't let you lay out two bucks for a hot dog, what makes you think I'll accept a thousand dollars, which I don't have a hope of paying back anytime in the near future?"

"Because this is an emergency," Harry said. "This is important."

"I can handle this myself. I would have had to handle it myself if you hadn't happened to hear the conversation in the first place."

"But I did," Harry said. "Things worked out the way they were supposed to. Don't be foolish, Acey."

The words weren't meant to sting, but they did. Acey flinched and sat down hard on the sofa. She looked around the room, her gaze roaming, not stopping anywhere. She needed to keep her eyes busy, because they were in danger of leaking, and she did not want to cry. "I can't do anything right," she said, mostly to herself. "Steph is my baby sister."

"She's no baby," Harry pointed out gently.

"I know, and generally she's more mature than I am, but she lives with me, and I still feel responsible for her happiness and health. And it's worked out all right. Some months are harder than others, bill-wise, but we usually manage, or can manage with extra hours at work." She felt a building pressure in her eyes, so she closed them and pressed her fingertips against her eyelids. "She loves that cat. I love that cat, too, but she *loves* that cat. And I can't help her. I can't even take care of a *cat*."

Harry knelt down beside her. She could feel the heat of his presence. "Please don't beat yourself up. Everyone screws up. Everyone has moments when they feel they disappointed someone, or hurt someone..." His voice caught. Acey opened her eyes, but Harry's head was turned away from her.

"I can do something for you to fix this," Harry said. "Please accept help. Please let me be the one you accept help from. Please."

Acey couldn't comprehend why his words sounded so plaintive, so desperate. "Why is it crucial to you that I say yes?"

After a pause, Harry said, "Because you'll be helping me just as much by saying yes."

At that moment, Acey remembered another time Harry had seemed mysteriously upset and distant—at the zoo, when he talked about a pet he had lost. Maybe it was a cat? Maybe giving her the money to save her pet would ease his pain?

No, wait. She couldn't believe she was seriously considering this offer. She'd never consider it from any other man. Probably not even her own father, if he'd had it to offer. "It's a lot of money," she said weakly.

"I know, but..." Harry's words trailed off, and then he started again. "Let's just say...let's just say I had a good month. I can afford it right now, as fate would have it."

A picture of that fate formed in Acey's head. The folded lottery ticket, stuck with a magnet to his refrigerator. Shimmering, sparkling, radiating.

Harry took her hand. He squeezed it, and she felt he needed her as much as she needed him.

"Okay," she finally said. "Okay." She blew a hard breath out of her mouth. "But we are paying you back as soon as possible."

"If you insist."

"I definitely do."

"All right." He sounded as if that wasn't ideal, but Acey wasn't going to agree to a gift. "How about ten dollars a week? Can you afford that payment plan?"

"I can double that, which still makes it a—" She did quick math in her head. "About a one-year loan. That's crazy."

"Why? Are you planning on dumping me as a friend?"

Acey thought of the day of the fake lottery winner, the day she was sure Harry was claiming the ticket. She remembered how she was certain Harry, a new rich playboy, wouldn't have time for her anymore. "Never. Are you?"

"Am I what? Thinking of dumping y'all as a friend?"

She nodded.

Harry looked incredulous. "And be out a thousand bucks? Are you nuts?" He appeared to hesitate, then put his arms around Acey. "Thank you."

Acey wrapped her arms around his solid body and put her face into the skin of his neck. "Hey, that's my line," she mumbled.

"Mine, too," Harry said.

Acey wanted to stay there, to forget everything but the safe spot she'd found. After a few minutes, however, it became clear to her that it was probably the least safe spot for her. She pulled away, but reluctantly. "You probably should go."

"Probably," he agreed. "But not before y'all fork over that essay. I'll go after I give it a peek. That is, if you don't mind."

"No," Acey said. "I mean, you just lent me a thousand bucks. I at least owe you an essay."

"Hey," Harry said sharply. "You don't owe me anything, except maybe one thousand bucks, and that's only because you insisted. You do what you want to do. Always. Do you understand?"

"Yeah." Acey stood. "That's what I want. I want you to read it."

"A'right, then."

Acey jogged to her bedroom, where Steph was lying on her bed, eyes closed, Sherlock draped over her middle. Acey tiptoed to her bed and picked up the paper.

"He's nice," Steph said.

"You scared me. I thought you were asleep."

"I was for a few minutes. He's nice, Acey. He doesn't need to share anything with us. He hasn't known you very long, and he doesn't know me at all."

"That's the way he is," Acey said. "I told you that when I first met him. He's a real toss-down-his-jacket-so-you-can-cross-a-puddle type."

"Yeah, but this was too much for charity. He cares about you."

The statement warmed Acey, but in her heart she also now knew that for some reason, Harry did this for himself. Not just today, but everything: carrying trash bags for the elderly, playing with kids, mediating between Steve and his girlfriend. Harry was purging a demon. Acey was mystified as to what that demon could be.

"He cares about you," Steph repeated, "but then again, a grand is the proverbial drop in the bucket for him now, eh?"

"Shh," Acey said, lowering her voice to a whisper. "Not unless he collects that prize," she pointed out. "And he hasn't."

"True."

"So that money is still his hard-earned cash," Acey whispered back.

"Maybe," Steph said, "but perhaps he's closer to collecting now. Excuse the pun, but perhaps your efforts are about to pay off for him. We thought he was the winner before, but this is evidence, isn't it?"

Acey closed the door firmly behind her.

Acey couldn't watch Harry read her essay. She thrust it at him and proceeded to pace into the kitchen, and out, and in, and out, for the few minutes it took him to read it. Which was minutes longer than it should have. What was he doing? Reading it four times? Was it that awful?

Finally, he laid the notebook down next to him. Acey rushed over and sat on the floor, looking up to him, like student to teacher. "Was it terrible?"

Harry blinked. "Absolutely not."

"Is it the kind of essay you would have written?" she demanded.

"Absolutely not," he repeated.

"Oh, no," Acey said. "Oh, no, I'll redo it. I'll work on it hard tonight and next time it will be better—"

"No," Harry cut her off. "I mean, it's not what I would have written because you're the only one who could have. The language, the feeling, it's all you. You put yourself out there. It's perfect. Do not change a word. Just type it up and send it."

Acey grabbed her notebook off the sofa and regarded it a bit disbelievingly. "You think they're going to like me?"

Harry stood and went to her front door. When his hand grasped the knob, she thought maybe he hadn't heard her, or maybe he didn't have an answer. Until he said, "They're going to love you."

Acey avoided calling Harry the next day, her day off, but she had to wrestle herself away from the phone several times. The tension was growing way too thick between them to risk alone time together.

She spent the day productively, however, by typing up her essay and mailing in an application. She was only brave enough to mail one at a time. She also sat with Steph while she called the vet and made an appointment for Sherlock for next week. When they hung up, Sherlock paused in the midst of licking himself to stare at them reproachfully.

"You just cost us a thousand dollars, buster," Acey said, but kindly.

That evening, Acey decided it might do her some good to learn a little about current events. After all, there was a very outside chance she might be returning to college, and she didn't want to sound as if she'd spent the past few years doing nothing but serving up pizza.

She settled in before the television, and learned that the Middle East was in turmoil, the Dow was down, and that after three weeks, the jackpot winner had still not surfaced.

"Where is he...or she?" the anchorwoman gleefully asked the camera, before reminding the viewers that legally, the winner had a year to claim the money.

"A year, huh?" Steph asked the screen from her spot on the floor. "More and more, it's looking that way. What's going on, Acey?"

"What?"

"Whaddaya mean, what? Whaddaya *think* I mean? Every time I think you made headway with that Harry, it yields nothing. What are you doing with him?"

"I told you, I'm trying. It's as if he knows what I'm up to, even though he doesn't. He kept wrecking everything by trying to tell me that money doesn't mean anything. Of course, I *know* it doesn't, but I can't *admit* that. Not when I'm trying to get him to take money. I thought he was about to claim the jackpot when he gave us the loan for the cat, because how could he afford it? But it looks like he'd rather take the financial hit than come forward. This is so *frustrating!*" Acey punched a sofa cushion, and managed to gouge her own palm with a long fingernail. "Ouch." She stood. "I need to be by myself," she said with some drama, and flounced off to her room.

"You'd better think of something!" her sister called.

Acey flopped on her bed, wanting to ignore her sister but afraid that she was right, that Acey-never-follows-through was lurking over her shoulder.

Think, Acey commanded herself. She had to admit she'd had pretty good ideas in the past though nothing had worked.

Now an idea was surfacing, and Acey had no choice but to mull it over: Tell Harry the truth. Tell Harry she knows he's the winner and just try to convince him friend to friend.

No. Maybe she could have broken down at the zoo, or at his apartment weeks ago, or some other time back at the beginning, but it just wasn't an option now. If she told him now, everything that had ever happened between them would seem to him manipulative, disingenuous. Especially since she had been stupid enough to kiss him. He'd think, well, he'd think what Charlie's family thought. That she'd sought him out just to hitch up to his gravy train. Then, maybe she'd make everything worse. Not only would Harry never speak to her again, but the revelation might be so hurtful that he definitely wouldn't claim his millions.

Acey sounded a little buzzer in her head. Sorry, wrong answer. Try again.

After about fifteen minutes of mental blankness, she was ready to give up.

Acey, she told herself, you can do more. You can be more. Be the Acey that is full of good ideas, the one who knocked Harry's socks off in Bread and Milk. The one who deserves that grant.

She rolled over onto her stomach and rubbed her temples. All right, so showing Harry the merits of money didn't work. What was stopping him? He thought money was bad? Why? He thought money made you into a bad person. What had he admitted to being afraid of? Becoming a different person.

Taking a risk.

That was it. Harry never took one damn risk. His apartment was spotless, practically lifeless, and he was always working. He lived the most risk-free life Acey had ever witnessed. So what did he need? He needed to learn to take risks. One big risk, specifically.

Acey was overjoyed to find that her brain could work logically if she consciously forced it to.

Right, so what would convince someone to take a big risk? By taking a smaller risk, and succeeding.

What could be a smaller risk?

Aha! Acey sat bolt upright, savoring the "aha!" moment. She wasn't sure she'd ever had one before, or maybe not such an obvious one. Her fingertips tingled.

A long time ago—well, only a few weeks ago, but it felt like a long time—Acey and Harry had been walking on Sunrise Highway, and he had mentioned, very casually, that he didn't ride horses and that he was afraid to.

One successful horseback ride was a small risk, and that was all he needed. Then he'd be full of confidence. Ready to tackle a bigger challenge, a bigger risk.

This could work!

If this didn't work…

Acey brushed away the pessimism. She'd make it work. She spied the cordless phone on Steph's bed and snatched it up. She dialed information and scrambled for a pen to take down a number.

Chapter Eleven

Acey parked Lydia's battered-but-borrowable Chevy, got out of the car and walked up to the office entrance before she realized Harry was not next to her. She looked over her shoulder, where he stood next to the car, frozen in place, searching her face. She doubled back.

"Hey," Acey said. "Surprise! We're going for a little trail ride."

"But..." Harry seemed to be struggling to put a sentence together, the right sentence that might make Acey say, *I was just kidding, let's get out of here.* His expression was stricken, unlike his playful demeanor the whole drive to Oyster Bay. He'd guessed a hundred places she could be taking him. "I...don't ride," he said now.

"I thought that's what you might have said once,"

Acey said. "I couldn't remember exactly." She crossed her fingers behind her back. "I have such good memories of trail rides with my parents, and I always wanted to do it again, and I was thinking, isn't now the perfect time, since I spend lots of free time with a cowboy? So I planned the surprise."

Well, yes, perhaps this was manipulative, but it was all for him in the end, Acey soothed herself. She was sure that appealing to him on her own behalf was better than appealing to him on his behalf. If she appeared to have not recalled his phobia, and framed this activity as something she really wanted for herself, Harry would be more likely to say yes, for her sake instead of his.

Watching his face, and the shadows that moved across it as he breathed raggedly through open, dry lips, Acey almost said, *Forget it, let's go home.* It was painful for her to see him so tortured over something that was, compared to other things he needed to face up to, so relatively small. She forced herself to wait, to give Harry one more minute to face his fears instead of avoiding them.

"All right," Harry said, in the quietest voice one could have above a whisper. "All right." He swallowed.

"It will be fun," Acey assured. "I know one of the guys in charge. I'm not a very experienced rider myself, so he's saddling up the two biggest sweeties in the stable. Completely harmless."

Harry nodded.

"We'll have a nice little ride, and then we'll go have some lunch." *Where you'll be so happy and proud of yourself for facing one fear that you'll be ready to do it again,* she added silently.

Harry merely nodded again.

Acey hesitated, and then held out her hand. Harry closed the distance between them with three steps and grasped her hand. Hard.

"Are you sure?" she whispered, against her better judgment. She didn't want to give him a chance to back out, but her heart hurt too much at his obvious terror.

"You brought us all the way here," Harry said. "It was your surprise. You really want to ride. Let's ride." His voice got slightly stronger with every sentence.

Hand in hand, Acey's heart thumping, they walked into the office. No one was there, so they went into the stable itself. Stalls lined either side of an aisle that was swept clean of hay and dirt. Acey could hear the horses snorting and shuffling in their stalls, as well as an occasional nicker, as if to say, *Here I am, in here.* Acey, hating to break the peaceful quiet, called out softly, then a little louder, "Dom? Dominic?"

There was a clatter below the floorboards, then heavy footsteps on stairs. A door to Acey's left swung open, and Dom stepped out. "Acey! Thought I heard yous."

"Hey, man," Acey said, throwing her arms around him in a good-natured hug. He patted her on the back, then after probably taking a good peek over her shoulder, said, "This the new guy we're trying to impress with a horse ride?"

Acey felt herself blush, but at least Dom's teasing appeared to have the effect of loosening Harry up a bit. "As if Acey needed to make an effort to impress anyone," he said. "Harry Wells."

"Dom D'Angelo," Dom answered. Harry studied Acey's old friend curiously, and Acey could certainly see why. At six foot three and generously over two hundred pounds, Dom looked more like a man accustomed to breaking up bar fights than breaking young horses. Dom had grown up on Acey's block. Back in high school, during one of his hooky-playing trips to Aqueduct Racetrack, he'd met some owners and fallen in love with the animals. Not gifted with racetrack savvy, Dom instead decided to work at various riding barns, taking to the hard work, and eventually became part owner of this stable. Acey'd never seen Dom actually riding a horse—she could only imagine the size of the horse that could carry him without collapsing—but she supposed the horses in his life found him to be as dependable as his human friends did.

"Let's get your horses tacked and ready to go," he said, walking them to the end of the aisle. "I don't remember you ever riding here, Acey."

"I haven't been riding since about junior high."

"What about you, Wells?" Dom asked.

"I don't ride," Harry replied, in a bit of a mumble.

"That's a'right. I got a coupla nice gentle ones for yous. They haven't been out yet today, so they should be happy. I'm having an unusually quiet day." He opened a stall door and led out a buttered-toast-colored horse, who looked even to Acey's untrained eye to be on the small side.

"This little palomino's named Flora," Dom said. "Small but sturdy. Perfect for my buddy Acey." He halted Flora in the middle of the aisle and clipped crossties to either side of her halter. Flora didn't so much as twitch an ear, and Acey had a feeling that if Dom had left her in the aisle without tying her, she would have stood just as still. Acey rubbed Flora's muzzle, amazed at how thin and soft the skin was. Flora closed her eyes.

Dom led a significantly larger horse out of an end stall, and cross-tied him behind Flora. "This is Jackson," he said, and the chestnut horse swished his lush tail as if to say, *That's my name, don't wear it out.*

"Don't let Jackson's size intimidate you," Dom said to Harry, whose expression Acey couldn't really read. "I haven't seen him go faster than a slow trot in about three years, and that's only if someone's holding out a bucket of carrots. He's twenty-seven, so we give him a break."

"Wow," Acey said. "Old man."

Harry caressed Jackson's neck a few times, then patted it. Jackson eyeballed him, as did Acey, but Harry seemed to be holding up all right. Probably a male stoicism thing, Acey thought, pretending he wasn't scared.

Dom handed Acey a small stiff-bristled brush, instructing her just how to groom Flora while he tacked up Jackson. She went to work on Flora, who took a deep, deep breath in and let it out, as if she were paying Acey a hundred dollars an hour for a spa treatment. Acey found the task just as relaxing herself. She used a softer brush on Flora's legs, keeping a distance from hooves. She didn't exactly have the confidence that came from experience with these large animals.

When she was done, Jackson was tacked up with a weighty-looking western saddle over a colorfully striped, folded blanket.

When Flora was saddled up, Dom instructed Acey and Harry to lead the horses outside. Acey wasn't quite sure how to go about it. She took two steps forward, taking slack from the reins, but Flora didn't budge. "Come on, girl," Acey cajoled, adding a "giddyap" to sound more cowgirlish. Flora rolled her eyes.

Dom clucked twice at Flora. "Get a move on," he said, and she reluctantly took a step, and then another. "I'll meet you guys out there," Dom said. "I gotta answer the phone real quick."

Acey led Flora outside, and stopped. Flora stopped with her, no problem. Acey turned and watched Harry lead Jackson from the barn. Jackson clomped heavier and shook his massive head when he emerged into the sun. Harry moved to the horse's left side, unbuckled the strap around the horse's stomach and pulled it tighter, rebuckling it.

"What are you doing?" Acey asked.

"I was, uh—" Harry said.

Dom emerged from the barn. "Sorry 'bout that. Okay. Now the first thing we do is tighten the girth straps on these guys. When you first tack a horse, you make it kinda loose. Eases them into it. After they walk a little and stretch, you tighten it a coupla notches. If you forget, the saddle could slip and you land on your ass."

He tightened Flora's girth as he talked, then went to Jackson. He slid a finger under the girth and said, "Huh, I guess that one's all right the way it is."

Acey looked at Harry, who was studying his boots.

Huh, indeed.

"Jilly's on her way out," Dom said. "She's one of my working students. I get a bunch of them when school's out for summer. She'll take you on the path. She knows her way around better than me anyway. All the kids do."

"You're not going with us?" Acey asked.

"Nah, I got too much to do around here. The little girls are great, but they can't do the heavy lifting. I'll see yous when you get back."

Dom moved closer to Acey and she whispered to him, "Make sure to tell me how much I owe you."

Dom patted her shoulder. "You owe me nothin'."

"Dom, you promised to let me pay you. Even though you would only agree to a discount rate."

"Just seeing an old friend is enough payment."

Dom cupped his hands together near her knee. He waited a minute, then looked up at her. "Well?"

"Well what?"

"Well, ya want a boost or not?"

"Oh, um…" She flailed her arms and legs around, trying to figure it out.

"Put your hands on the saddle," Dom said. "Put your foot in my hands. The *other* foot. What a city girl. Okay, hop up on three. One, two, three." He hoisted her into the saddle easily.

He turned to Harry, but Harry was already in the saddle. Longer legs, Acey thought.

She heard a clop-clopping and when she turned, she saw a beautiful Asian-American girl, who appeared to be no older than twelve, leading a tall, dark, jumpy-looking horse. "Hi," she said shyly, before vaulting onto the horse's back in one athletic motion. Acey was impressed.

"That's Jilly," Dom said. Then, he said to Jilly, "Isn't Comet a little spooky on the trails?"

"Not the last two times," Jilly said. "I've been working with him."

"If you say so. Be careful anyway. Take these two around the nice, long way."

"Don't you need help untacking the group coming back?" Jilly asked, frowning. Acey wondered if, at that age, she herself had developed that sense of responsibility to a job. She didn't think so. She just remembered wanting boys to ask for her phone number.

"I'll graze 'em till you get back, and you can deal with them then." Then he said to Harry and Acey, "Riding One-O-One. Reins in one hand. Move them right, turn right. Left, turn left. Back, halt. Lean forward going uphill and lean back going downhill. There, you've graduated. Any problems, Jilly will help yous."

Acey, trying desperately to commit the instructions to memory, glanced back at Harry, who was holding the reins in one hand, his other hand resting easily on his thigh. His face was tense and unsmiling, but the rest of his body looked as though he was born and raised on a horse.

Hmm.

Jilly clucked once at Comet and moved ahead onto a dirt path.

"Let Jackson follow Comet," Dom called, "and let Flora go last. She hates other horses close on her heels, and besides, if Jackson is last, he may end up a mile behind yous."

Acey turned in the saddle again and saw Harry's eyes closed. Which would probably be an extrarisky way to ride. After a few seconds, he opened them, squared his shoulders—which, Acey tried not to notice, gave him a prince-on-horseback kind of look—and nudged the horse underneath him forward.

Jackson came around Acey's left, close enough that Harry's blue-jeaned leg brushed her own. She felt the heat of his skin, and felt her own heat pound through, right around the area of the saddle. "Whoa, girl," she said softly, and not to Flora.

They crossed a gravelly parking lot and moved through an open gate, single file, until they were on a dirt path in a clearing. A little farther along, they were soon in the midst of the woods, and it was cooler and darker here as the treetops blocked the direct sunlight. Flora paused every few steps to chew off clumps of leaves at the side of the narrow trail. Acey admonished her softly and ineffectively, and soon gave up. She switched her attention to Harry.

The lower half of his body swayed gracefully with Jackson's every stride. Acey didn't understand it, because her behind bumped against the hard saddle with *her* horse's every stride. She would have thought Ma's stuffed shells and eggplant parmigiana all these years had padded her rear enough, but no luck. It was the first time, and likely the last, that she wished her butt was bigger.

The trio—or sextet, if the four-legged companions were counted—moved along quietly for about a half hour, the only noises an occasional bird or a branch brushing against their legs as they passed. Acey grew drowsy. Between her family and her job, she was unaccustomed to tranquility.

Flora clearly could walk this trail in the middle of the night with one eye closed, so Acey allowed herself to daydream, anticipating Harry's pride and satisfaction when this ride was over and declared a success. She predicted that by dinnertime, he'd be confessing his lottery win and plotting his future.

Just then, in the exact moment Acey was planning how she'd managed to look shocked, fate handed her a real shock.

A shout. Followed by a female giggle. Flora's ears pricked.

To Acey's right, an unidentified flying object sailed out of the trees.

Comet, caught off guard by the sudden red blur, shrieked and reared slightly. Acey jumped a little, startled by the reaction. Jilly clutched a fistful of mane to avoid being dumped backward as Comet bounced his front legs up and down, up and down, snorting raggedly. Wary Jackson shifted to the left edge of the trail, clearing an unfortunate space in front of Flora. Unfortunate because, as Comet screamed a whinny again, Flora, sensing it was panic time, pitched forward. Acey grabbed the reins tight in both hands, which had no effect except to agitate the mare more.

Flora bolted.

She bolted past Jackson, pushed aggressively past Comet and, with nothing but open space before her, ran for her life.

She only ran faster when Acey screamed.

"Y'all stay here," Harry commanded Jilly.

"But—"

"I said stay here. Don't move." He hesitated for less than a split second, Belle's death cry echoing in his memory, then dug his heels into Jackson's flanks, snapped the end of the reins across the animal's shoulders and shouted a wordless yelp. Jackson drove forward into a steady gallop.

"But you don't know what you're doing!" Jilly called after Harry.

But he *did* know.

Flora was in freak-out mode, but old man Jackson's legs covered more ground. Soon Harry was close enough.

Inexperienced Acey, who didn't know the first thing about equitation, was jolting around in the saddle, her legs flopping. He could hear her shouting "whoa," but it sounded more like "whoa-oa-oa!"

Flora dived off the trail into an open clearing.

"Acey!" Harry yelled.

"Harr-rrr-rry!"

"Don't panic! Use the reins! Pull left! Pull hard to the left!"

He could see her tugging.

"Pull harder! Pull her whole head to the left!"

He worried that the wind rushing in her ears would block his instructions, but she obeyed. Flora veered a sharp left.

"Keep pulling! Force her into a circle! She can't gallop fast in a circle!"

Acey kept tugging, and Flora began to spiral around herself. Her legs tripped over each other and she slowed, slowed, slowed. Harry and Jackson skidded to a stop beside them and Harry took hold of Flora's bridle. The mare tossed her head once, affronted, then halted completely, panting.

Her rider was panting, too. Her hands were shaking and her fingers were white, clutched around the reins. Harry took the leather straps from her and she put her face into her hands.

"Relax," Harry said. "It's really scary. Y'all didn't even run that far, but it sure feels like forever when you're riding helpless."

Flora's breathing began to slow, but she was still sweating profusely. Jackson, on the other hand, was barely fatigued. "Got a little more energy in you than anyone thought, eh?" Harry asked, patting his neck. "Good job, old man. Full of surprises."

"Yeah," Acey said flatly. "Full of surprises." It wasn't

Jackson she was addressing, however. "Thanks for saving my life," she continued in the same toneless voice.

"I didn't. At worst, maybe, I saved you from a broken bone."

"The point is, *you* saved me. Which is very interesting. Don't you think?"

Busted.

Jilly and Comet cantered out into the clearing to join them. "Are you all right?"

"She's fine," Harry said. "Everyone's fine." Except maybe me, he added silently.

"You were brave, mister," Jilly said, then added, almost to herself, "Dom's gonna *kill* me."

"No, he won't," Harry replied. "The best-trained horses get spooked sometimes."

"You should listen to him," Acey said. "He's an expert."

Harry looked at Acey. "Apparently," she added.

"It's fine," Harry said to Jilly. "We'll tell Dom what happened."

"Do you guys want to keep riding or head back?" Jilly asked.

Acey slid off Flora. Harry noticed her knees wobbling as she landed. "I think Flora's had it for the day," she said, rubbing the mare between the ears. "I know I have. I'm sorry about this, Jilly. I was having a great time until something came flying. Was it…?"

"A Frisbee," Harry confirmed. "Kids playing in the woods, no doubt."

Jilly turned Comet and began a slow pace back to the trail. Harry hopped off Jackson to lead him beside Acey and Flora. Acey patted Jackson and murmured, "Thanks," to him. Harry smiled, but the smile wasn't half complete before Acey shot him a look that faded it.

"I really am grateful for your help," she said in a low voice so their guide wouldn't hear. "But if you don't mind, go on ahead of us. I just don't want to talk to you right now."

Stung, Harry nodded and moved ahead of her. Every few feet, though, he turned to make sure she was all right. Every time he did, she saw him and pretended not to.

It hurt. Just like he'd known it would.

Chapter Twelve

After returning to the barn and explaining everything to Dom, who determined that everyone was okay, Acey and Harry drove home in silence. Acey didn't even bother to turn on the radio, and the hypnotic hum of wheels on road became unbearable for Harry.

It was going to be difficult enough to reveal some of his truth. Not having an open-minded audience would only make it worse. Acey was angry that he lied, and he couldn't blame her, after all she'd shared. Friendship was a two-way street. Not to mention their particular friendship-plus-some, which should have been a two-way street with several lanes.

Acey eased the car into a metered spot in front of Focaccia's and slipped out to drop quarters in the meter and return the keys to Lydia. When she emerged alone a few minutes later, Harry assumed she'd not confided his lie to her friends, who were protective enough to have come out and knocked him around if she had.

Acey looked through him, expressionless, as if he could have been a mailbox on the curb beside the car. Then she turned on her heel and walked up the street.

Harry jogged a little to catch up to her. She walked along, not saying anything or turning her head, and soon hung another right that took her off course for both of their apartments.

He followed.

Not breaking stride, Acey said, "You live the other way."

"I want to talk to you."

"Oh, now you want to talk to me?" She shook her head, her straight-ahead focus never wavering. "As if you haven't had all the time in the world to tell me things about yourself. I had to drag practically every teeny, tiny detail out of you, and there weren't many. Now you're actually volunteering information?"

"Yes."

She stopped and pivoted to face him. "You told me you were afraid to ride."

"Yeah."

"But you're *not* afraid to ride."

"Actually, I was afraid to ride. But I never said I didn't know how to ride. I was just afraid to."

"I do *not* want to play stupid word games with you. You lied."

"Yeah."

Acey shrugged. "Whatever." She resumed walking.

Harry kept on her heels. "What do you mean, 'whatever'?"

"Exactly that. Whatever. You don't owe me the truth. You don't owe me anything. After all I've done for you..." She checked herself and restarted. "I mean, after all the times I put myself out there with you, telling you about Charlie, and my dropping out of school, and all this personal stuff, you didn't tell me squat. I thought you were just superprivate and I respected that. But..."

"But you can't respect a lie," Harry finished for her. "And the horse thing was a lie."

"Yeah, and it was such a weird lie, I don't know what to think. Or if I should think anything. It seems like I should, though."

"Yeah, you should."

Their directionless walk had led them to the edge of the Village Green, a vast expanse of healthy grass that ended at the public library. Harry took Acey's stiff hand, and she didn't curl it around his. He tugged on it anyhow.

"Come with me."

The last of the daylight barely filtered through the leaves overhead, transforming the public park into a more shadowy and private place. Harry pulled a dragging Acey up to the gazebo on the Green, and sat on the top step, pulling her down to sit beside him.

He let go of her hand then. After he told her his story, it would be her choice whether or not to ever touch him again.

"Before I left Texas...well, I had an accident. It was a bad accident, and I was completely at fault."

"I thought accidents were called accidents because they're no one's fault," Acey said and, despite the task before him, Harry smiled. Even when she was about to get the confession she had practically demanded, Acey couldn't help interrupting.

"This one was," Harry continued, sobering as Belle's striking form pieced together in his mind. "It was about a year ago. I was in a show-jumping competition. Grand prix level."

"Does grand prix mean you were supergood?"

"I was supernervy, at the very least. Anyway, I didn't have a horse ready to compete at that level."

"Probably too expensive," Acey murmured.

Harry felt a pang but let that one go, or he'd never finish. "I didn't have a horse at that level," he repeated, "but my girlfriend did."

"Girlfriend?" Acey seemed to not know what reaction to have to the word, and as a result, her face twisted strangely.

"Less of a girlfriend and more like the woman I was spending the most time with," Harry clarified, unsure if the explanation helped any. "Lara. She was nice enough. Fun. We had…a lot in common. It was definitely mutual that it wasn't a permanent thing. But that was no reason to use our friendship like I did."

"What do you mean?"

"She had a grand prix horse, Belle. Belle of the Ball. This horse was phenomenal. She moved like a tall, cool glass of water. The only thing was, Lara was a solid rider, but not as good as me."

"You convinced her to let you ride Belle in the competition," Acey guessed.

"I had to talk Lara into it. I shouldn't have. If she'd agreed right away, it would have been one thing, but she wasn't sure if my ability was quite what I made it out to be. As it turned out, she was right. It wasn't."

Acey waited.

A drop of perspiration eased down the side of Harry's face, despite the cooling evening air. He swiped it away with one finger. "Belle, she...we crashed at a fence. It was my fault. I was anticipating the fence beyond it, and she didn't feel confident, I guess. See, horses can sense if you're not all there with them. Their eyes are in the sides of their heads, so the last stride to the fence, they actually can't see it. If they don't feel your confidence, they hesitate, or refuse the fence."

"She refused?"

"I wish she had, because then I would have been the only one who got hurt."

Something blocked Harry's throat, cutting off his words. He put a hand to his face, but when he breathed in, Jackson's scent lingered on his skin and the horse smell worsened the pain.

"She fell," Harry finally said, knowing he didn't have the strength to elaborate with details. "On top of me. She hit her skull and died."

"Oh, Harry," Acey said, aghast. "Oh, no."

Harry couldn't speak again. Eventually he became aware that he was moving, and realized Acey had encircled him with her arm and was rocking him. Her eyes were closed, and her brows squashed together, as if she was concentrating on absorbing his hurt.

Because she was sharing his burden now, he could say more of it out loud. "It was because of me, my selfishness. She was this amazing horse, talented and all heart. She loved people, she loved Lara."

"Poor Lara," Acey said. "Poor Belle. Poor you."

The irony of her phrasing cut like a dagger. "No. Certainly not poor me."

"You didn't get hurt?"

"I did get hurt. There's a pin in my knee, but you know, that was the least of it all. I've gotten hurt before doing crazy daredevil things."

"Well, that's what guys do, right?"

"No," Harry said. His voice trembled. He tried to control it and failed. "A living creature died because of me. I tried to make it right the only way I could think of. I offered to get Lara another horse."

"You couldn't do that. Way too expensive."

"Well, she refused." He wiped his face again with his sleeve. "I didn't love Lara, but she was my friend, and hurting her like that was the worst thing I've ever done. I never want to do that again, be like that again."

Acey pulled back as a revelation occurred to her. "Sherlock. That's why you lent us the money. You're still doing penance."

Harry nodded wearily. "I would have wanted to lend you the cash anyway because you're my friend, but yeah, that was part of it."

"And that's why you're so extra helpful and good to everyone. To try to make up for your past?"

Harry dropped his voice to a whisper. "To be a different person."

"You're not a different person," Acey said. "You're the same person who endured something terrible and is trying to change." She stroked his hair, and the brush of her long nails on his scalp made him shiver.

"I was terrified today," Harry admitted.

"Of course you were."

"I never wanted to be responsible for another horse ever again. When Dom brought Jackson out, I thought, maybe I can do this. He was such an old, slow guy and we were just taking a walk. Then you and Flora…and I actually hesitated before chasing you. I was so afraid of injuring a horse, but the thought of *you* being hurt overrode every other concern in my head."

"Jilly was right," Acey said, leaning over until her cheek touched his. "You were brave, mister." She paused, and Harry's face felt her face tighten as she smiled. "For me. You were brave for me."

She moved her hand to his face, laying her palm against his skin. Her own skin was cool and forgiving.

Harry slid his fingers down her bare forearm and took hold of her hand. Acey turned to him, her face less than centimeters from his. Harry lifted her hand to his lips and pressed his mouth against her open palm. Her fingertips brushed his brow and eyelids. He kept his lips there, tasting her softness, until he heard her emit a small sound from her throat. He opened his eyes and peeked between her fingers to see her face slackened in surrender, her eyes half-closed, her lips parted.

He ended the intimate kiss with a tiny touch of his tongue on a crease in her hand.

Harry might have been able to stop there, but she made that sound again, a sound that escaped with no form, no meaning. Just emotion.

He wanted, needed, to hear it again.

He slid her ring finger into his mouth, licking the inside length up and down, then swirling his tongue around the pad on the end. When he pulled her finger out, he let it drag against his lower lip all the way.

No longer willing or able to fight the urge to kiss Acey, Harry leaned in. She leaned in at the same time, with matching fervor, so when their mouths met, it was with a bruising, teeth-knocking intensity that took his breath away. They parted their lips and slid their tongues together in a kiss that wasn't tentative or exploratory. It was a greedy, hungry kiss, a kiss that demanded—

"More," Acey said, her mouth pressing the word into his mouth.

He agreed, "More."

She made that sound.

He eased the top half of her body down until they were half lying on the floor of the gazebo. Her hair spread out like a dark halo, and Harry buried his face in the strands, inhaling that achingly familiar raspberry scent. He brushed his lips against her earlobe, nibbled it, working the delicate skin between his teeth before trailing kisses down her jawline. When he reached her chin, he pulled back to look at her.

Her eyes were heavy-lidded, her skin flushed in the yellow glow of the nearest streetlamp. The side of her face, where he had just been lavishing his attention, was moist, and there was a sheen of lust across her forehead.

Acey locked her gaze onto his, and yanked the hem of her T-shirt from her jeans. She grabbed both his wrists, nails digging, and pulled his hands toward her. When he felt her bare flesh, he was amazed his fingers didn't sizzle and drop off. She was warm. No, she was hot.

He smoothed his palms up her sides. When he reached the barrier of her bra, he unworked the front clasp and her breasts fell heavy into his hands.

Maybe she made that sound again. He didn't know, because he only heard himself make that sound.

He brushed his thumbs over her nipples, which were already as hard as glass. He fumbled with his elbows a bit to push her shirt up, and she assisted by lifting it to her chin. Her breasts were round and perfect, and he bent his head to taste one.

Acey threw back her head and moaned. Harry glanced up as taillights from a passing car illuminated the pleasure on her face. He licked a tight nipple once more and lowered her shirt.

Acey's expression changed from ecstatic to confused.

"I want you," Harry said, to erase any misunderstanding. "But I want you in private. I want you in my bed. I don't want to be looking around to see if anyone's passing by. I want to see nothing but your face as we make love, over and over."

Acey's eyes widened.

"If that's all right with you, of course," Harry added with a soft smile.

"Let's go," Acey said, sitting up and raking her thick hair back. "Let's go now. But let's not…I don't want to talk."

Harry raised a questioning brow.

"We've done a lot of talking," Acey said. "It's not time for that right now. It's time for this. You want me. And I want you. Badly. If we say anything more, it could…"

"Break the spell."

Acey nodded and kissed him. Her lips were moist and hot.

She broke it off, breathing hard, and Harry nodded in acquiescence. He grasped her hand and they helped each other stand. Then he began walking. She matched his pace, even when he quickened it.

After a block or two, Harry felt the pang of the truth

Acey still didn't know about him. He briefly considered breaking their promise of silence but couldn't. One truth at a time. Acey was right. It was time for this—to face the truth of their own bodies, their need to have each other. It was as real a truth as any. There would be time for another truth tomorrow.

Tomorrow, Acey thought, panting a little but refusing to slow down. Tomorrow was soon enough to tell Harry she knew about him, and to admit what she'd originally been up to. For tonight, they'd be honest in a different way, in a long-overdue way.

Her blood thumped in her ears, in her heart, and down between her legs. She staggered against Harry, who slipped his arm around her waist and guided her toward his apartment where, in his bed, some naked secrets would be revealed.

After some fumbling around with the key, nearly prompting Acey to break their silence with a curse, the door swung open. The two fell into the living room, landing on the floor with a thud, their arms entwined around each other. They resumed fumbling, but this time it was deliberate.

Harry kicked out his foot to slam the door, and winced.

"Your knee!" Acey gasped, between desperate kisses.

"It's fine," he said. "My knee's not what's aching, darlin'."

She rubbed her cheek against the side of his face, scratching her skin on his abrasive yet sexy stubble. She clutched at his chest, coming up with only fistfuls of cotton shirt. She pulled away from his embrace with a mighty effort, and tore the shirt over his head.

He scooted backward, tugging her along, pulling off her shirt and tossing it over her shoulder.

They moved down the hall like that, half crawling, half scooching, pausing only to kiss and discard items of unwanted clothing like a sensual breadcrumb trail to the bedroom.

Flat on her back on the floor, the bed seemed like an ambitious climb, but before Acey could consider the best route, Harry hoisted her up, leaving her legs dangling over the edge. She had on only her bra and panties, and expected Harry to join her to remove them, but after a long moment, she was still alone.

"Hey," she protested, then felt Harry's fingers wrap around her ankles. "There you are," she breathed as he ran his tongue along the instep of her right foot.

He worked his way up her leg, licking a trail for his fingertips to follow. He kissed her knee and draped her leg over his shoulder as he traveled up her inner thigh, pausing several times to nibble and suck until Acey nearly grabbed his head with both hands and put him where she wanted him.

Suddenly, he *was* where she wanted him.

His mouth was hot, covering her, with only the thin, damp nylon of her panties between them. He pretended the fabric didn't exist, and she soon forgot it was there, until he paused to slip his hands inside the waistband and slide them down her legs. He bent down to her again, and the heat of the intimacy made Acey cry out.

His tongue parted her folds to find the tiny nub at her center, which he drew in between his lips and out again, and in and out.

Acey saw stars. And colors. She inclined her head so she could see him. His eyes were on her face, his steady attention assuring her he wouldn't stop before he brought her to ultimate satisfaction.

He didn't need to keep the unspoken promise for long.

She exploded, shattered, with a cry she didn't hear until a moment after she uttered it, its echo reverberating back at her.

She jerked involuntarily away from his mouth, too sensitive now for him to even breathe on her. Harry obliged by backing away, but only for about two seconds, before he was bracing himself above her, pressing his hard length against her tingling dampness.

He groaned, and Acey reveled in the sound, marveled that she was the one who drew it out of him.

"I can't… Acey, I can't stop," Harry said hoarsely.

"Who the hell asked you to?" she replied, grabbing his ass—his amazingly tight, firm ass—in both hands.

He plunged into her in one swift motion, burying himself so completely their bodies crashed against each other.

Then he pulled out again almost as abruptly.

Acey nearly screamed in frustration. Harry put his face next to her ear, nudging a lock of hair out of the way with his nose.

"Sorry," he whispered. "I couldn't wait to feel you. I had to. Now, I'll do it right."

"It seemed more than right to me," Acey said, "but I'll…oh, yeah…I'll just…mmm…take your word for it."

Harry sank into her, but this time it was *slow.* His skin was slippery from his first dip inside, adding to Acey's slickness. When he was almost all the way in, Acey wrapped her legs around his back. She squeezed with her thighs and pulled him in so hard, the blankets slipped and they pushed against the wall. Harry quickly placed his hand behind her so the crown of her head ran into his protective open palm.

He scrunched her hair in his hand as he thrust in and out.

All gentleness was abandoned, by silent mutual consent. They had waited too long for this, and so they thrust together over and over. Acey watched his face, anticipating being witness to his moment of release. She sensed its approach, but without warning, her own blood began to swirl hot in her feminine core, burning and insisting on more, more—again.

The sensation spiraled up, and her gaze followed it to the ceiling as she gasped. Harry pressed into her one last hard time and unleashed an animal groan. The first hot throbs of his climax pushed her own over the edge.

They lay still for many minutes. The spasms ebbed away, with Acey trying and failing to separate which were hers and which were his.

Harry rolled onto his side but took Acey with him, not pulling out of her. He brushed her sweaty, damp hair from her face, and they regarded each other for the first time not as friends, and not as friends who both secretly longed for something more, but as the something more. It felt warmer, thicker, and more—right.

"Acey," Harry said haltingly. "That was… I never… You were… *We* were…"

"I know," Acey said. *I know. I know about you. I know your truth. I know I have to tell you mine. I know no one has ever made me feel this way. I know this can work out.*

Did she really?

"I know," she murmured again, allowing the night to

come to a close. She kissed each of his delicate eyelids shut as he drifted off to sleep.

Tomorrow, Acey reminded herself, curling into him, her face against his chest. Tomorrow, everything will be all right.

Ralph Wakefield wasn't hanging around at this hour of the night at the *New York Transcript* office because he didn't have better things to do. He did.

Okay, fine. He was here because he didn't have better things to do. Because he was boring. Because although he worked at an exciting tabloid in New York City, he had a distinctly *unexciting* job in the business department. He didn't get to dog celebrities and ask them questions about their love lives. He didn't get to expose the seamy underside of politics. He didn't even get press passes to the Yankees games, for crying out loud. He worked for the section of the paper slammed by the rest of the staff as *boring*.

He'd begged, pleaded, cajoled—hell, even *whined*—to the managing editor to throw him a general-assignment bone. But no luck. The editor had said he didn't see anything in Ralph's work that made him believe the business scribe belonged on the other side of the newsroom.

In other words, his stories were boring.

So he fed his desire for more by hanging around late once in a while—okay, all five nights of the week. He dealt with nine-to-five businesspeople, so technically his work could be turned in by six, and always was. He never missed a deadline. But he couldn't bring himself to leave. He enjoyed watching the news reporters scuttle around like busy ants, especially when there was a breaking story. Ralph could acknowledge it was pathetic, living vicariously through his colleagues.

He didn't care. He'd get over there someday. He just needed a break.

"Yo," Ralph heard behind his shoulder.

"Yo," Ralph said back, looking up from a trade magazine he often used to appear knee-deep in research after hours. Aaron flopped in a creaky desk chair on the other side of Ralph's desk. "What are you doing here?" Ralph asked his friend. "You don't work tonight."

"Ah, just wanted to develop some film," Aaron said, propping his sandals on the desk. Ralph tried to avoid looking at his feet. Aaron tossed a few black-and-white photos on the desk. "If I leave any pictures in the camera, I forget all about 'em."

Upside down, Ralph could see horses. And a very beautiful, panicky woman. He slid the picture closer. "She's on a runaway horse."

"Yup," Aaron said. "I got a couple of good photos. I had to run like hell to get a good shot. That horse was really moving, spooked by a flying Frisbee. But this guy helped her out, yelled instructions to her, slowed her down."

"Why didn't you turn 'em in?"

"Eh, they're nice pictures, but space is too tight in the paper these days for pics with no real story. No one died, and it's not as if she's anyone famous."

Ralph picked up the first photo and studied the second one. Studied the man holding on to the horse's head as the female rider cradled her own head in relief.

"Aaron," Ralph said conversationally, "you ever read the business section of our own paper?"

"Nah, man, that crap's too boring. No offense."

Ralph raised an eyebrow.

"I don't read any of our paper," Aaron said, as if this information was any more comforting. "I just look at my pictures. And read the comics."

"Don't let the editors hear you say that. My point is, if you read the business section, you'd know this man *is* famous."

"I *thought* he looked like Matthew McConaughey."

"No, doofus. His name is Harrison Wells."

Aaron was a blank.

"Heir to a humongous Texas ranching business?"

Still blank.

"I haven't heard anything about him in about a year," Ralph said. "He had an accident. Come to think, it was actually some kind of horse-riding accident."

"Well," Aaron finally said. "That would make the picture newsworthy."

"You need to confirm it. Where was this?"

"North Shore. I was on a little picnic thing with my girlfriend. *Her* idea."

"So he's on the North Shore?"

"Nah, we parked near the barn, and when we went to the car, I heard a couple of the barn people talking, this huge guy and this kid, a girl. They were talking about the couple."

"Do you remember anything?"

Aaron thought. "Mentioned Valley Stream."

"Maybe he moved there," Ralph said. "I'll track him down."

"Yeah?"

"Yeah, those pictures will be fresh for at least another day." Ralph stood and gathered his things. No need to hang around here. He had his own story to chase, for a change. "By the way, did the horses run right by your picnic blanket?"

"No." Aaron was sheepish. "I threw the Frisbee."

"You're kidding."

"My girlfriend's great at Frisbee, but I'm not."

"Clearly." Ralph sighed, meaning it to sound like a world-weary sigh, but he was eager to start working. "I'll find Wells," he promised. "Tomorrow."

Chapter Thirteen

When Harry left to fetch breakfast, Acey was fast asleep, her hair covering her pillow and part of his. Looking at her, Harry almost couldn't leave the bed. It didn't make sense to not want to be exactly where Acey Corelli was at every moment. But he knew they had to eat, so he tore himself away.

When he returned, bags in hand, Acey was up and out. Harry called her name, and she rapped on the window from out on his porch. He stared out at her. She was wearing one of his button-down shirts. It just barely covered her behind. Her legs poured out from under the hem, long and ripe and perfect, ending in bare toes. She bent down and waved his attention back to her face, acknowledging that she was being ogled. *Sorry*, Harry mouthed. What a pig he was. Thank goodness for him,

Acey just laughed and turned around, looking out at the street.

The wind teased the shirt around her skin. Harry was ecstatic that she was here, but remembered that he needed to come clean to her. He thought—he hoped—that it would all be okay. He knew she didn't want a rich man, but now that she'd gotten to know and possibly developed strong feelings for Harry the person, maybe she could let that restriction go. He knew she might be angry he hadn't told her until now, but he'd tell her that he wanted to change her mind about money being important, and show her how to get things and enjoy life without it, and he just couldn't tell her then.

She had said last night that he didn't owe her the truth. That was arguable, but this morning, he damn well owed her the truth. He'd deliver it with tenderness and…maybe best to tell her while he was naked. Hmm. Better play it by ear, he decided.

He nudged open the porch door and stepped out with bags. "Acey, you are a vision."

"I'm a wreck. Don't look at me. My hair is like a wasp's nest. I slept in my eye makeup and now I resemble a raccoon on a bender."

Harry put his free arm around her shoulders, pulled her close and kissed her deeply. "Mmm, minty fresh."

"Yeah, I used your toothbrush."

"Gross."

Acey shoved him.

"Just kidding. Look, bagels." He spread breakfast out on the table with one hand, not letting go of his hold on her.

"Bagels! Getting to be a real New Yorker, eh, cowboy?"

"Y'all better believe it."

"Huh. Never mind."

"Hey, is your sister going to worry about you?"

"I think she'll guess what happened."

Harry finished setting the table and put both arms around her. "I was going to give you breakfast in bed, but you got up."

"I'll have something to eat in bed later, then."

Harry felt himself grow hard. Make that harder. There hadn't been a moment in weeks with Acey when he wasn't hard at just her nearness.

Acey ran her fingers down his chest, reached his belt and unbuckled, never taking her eyes off his. "I don't think anyone can see us if we stand a couple of feet back," she said conversationally. "It's pretty early on a Sunday morning anyhow. No one will see if I..." She unzipped his jeans and yanked them down over his hips. "If I..." She tantalized, sliding a finger underneath the waistband of his briefs and pulling them down as well. "If I..." she whispered, and sank to her knees.

"Acey," Harry groaned as she took him into her mouth. She slid her tongue up and down and around. She tugged with her lips, gently, then not so gently, then back to gently.

"Acey," Harry said, louder, fast approaching total loss of control. Without warning, Acey pushed away from him, turned around and rose back up to her feet. Slowly. Rubbing her bare self against his legs all the way up, and bucking her hips once.

Harry grabbed hold of her hips, and Acey braced her hands on the table, bending over. Just the sight of her made Harry nearly lose his mind, but out of sheer determination, he held off until she pressed into him, and onto him.

Acey threw her head back, resting it on Harry's shoulder. He reached up and turned her head, kissing her, tasting her mouth as she settled against him. She took his other hand and placed it on her breast. He flicked his thumb over her nipple, and when it elicited a moan, he did it again.

Then she trailed her hand down her own body, between her breasts and over her stomach, and touched herself, and him. Harry grabbed hold of both her hips again and thrust into her over and over, and she met every thrust with a rocking motion of her own, until they came together in a blast of passion and heat.

They stopped moving, and Harry dropped his head onto her back.

"Now," Acey finally said, "I think we officially woke up the neighborhood."

Harry dragged himself away from her. When she turned to face him, he kissed her again and realized how close he was to saying it, saying something he'd never said to a woman.

Something, he told himself, that would have to wait until she knew everything. He tried to make it up to her with a smile that said it.

Acey regarded him. "Wow."

"Wow what?"

"Wow, wow. I don't know, just wow." She headed for the bedroom. "I'm going to put some clothes on."

"Don't do that on my account."

"I'm doing it on mine. If I don't get some clothes on, it would be just too easy to make love to you again and then I'll never eat."

"So?"

"So no food equals no strength to make love again. Got it?"

"That would be a tragedy. By all means, dress."

They ate bagels, drank orange juice, and before nine o'clock, the day was already perfect.

"I've got something to talk to you about," Harry said.

Acey froze for a moment. "Sounds serious."

"Kind of."

"I actually have something to talk to you about, too, and I think it's probably a related topic."

"How would you know that?"

"Intuition. In fact, intuition is what started the whole thing."

"What do you mean?"

"You go first."

They leaned forward at the same time for a kiss. When they separated, Harry took a deep breath and hoped his nervousness wasn't obvious. "Okay, here's the thing."

Acey leaned forward expectantly.

Harry opened his mouth, and the doorbell buzzed.

"That was a neat trick," Acey said. "Can you do it again?"

Harry jumped up. "I asked the delivery kid to buzz on Sundays with the newspaper because someone's been stealing mine when he leaves it on the front step. Be right back."

He dashed into the living room and buzzed on his end. He expected the kid to leave it in the foyer, but he heard footsteps on his stairs. Was it the week to pay? He didn't think so.

Acey materialized behind him. "It's chilly out. I'm staying here."

"Okay. Hold on." There was a knock, and Harry swung the door open, fumbling for his wallet.

"Mr. Wells?"

Harry looked up from his fumbling. This was no kid. A man stood on his step, with a perfectly pressed shirt and blue silk tie. Maybe this was the kid's father? Had he forgotten to pay last week and the kid had sent his father over to collect?

"Yes?"

"Mr. Harrison Wells?"

Harry gave a start. "Yes?" he asked again, but a little more sharply. The man appeared somewhat overeager, considering Harry only owed a few bucks.

"I'm Ralph Wakefield, *New York Transcript*?"

Harry shook his head. "You must be looking for one of my neighbors. I subscribe to the *Times*."

"No, I'm definitely looking for you," Ralph Wakefield said with a bit of a smirk. "And I'm not the only one. Apparently your family doesn't know quite where you are, either."

Harry should have slammed the door in Ralph Wakefield's face, but the statement was so shocking it took a few seconds to register. In those few seconds, Acey moved close behind Harry's shoulder.

"Harry? What's going on?" Acey asked.

"I thought I'd track you down," Ralph said, "since I got wind of a little story about you."

Harry shook his head, and kept shaking it.

Acey's eyes widened. *New York Transcript.* Tracking Harry down. Little story.

She had no idea how on earth this Ralph guy could have found out anything, but the timing was perfect. Harry'd been about to tell her anyway. He'd opened his mouth to say it. It was fate!

She tugged urgently at his shirt. "Harry," she whispered. He didn't turn around. "Harry," she said, louder. When he still didn't move, she pulled on his shoulder until he half turned to face her. "Tell him," she said.

"What?"

"Tell him," Acey said. "Get it out in the open. It's all right. You don't have to be afraid."

"Afraid?" Ralph asked, but Acey ignored him.

"Tell him the truth," Acey said. "Embrace your future. It's an unbelievable gift. You deserve it. It will all be okay. If you need me to do anything to help you, I will."

"What are y'all talking about?" Harry asked, turning completely around now to face her.

"You know," Acey said. "And I know, because I figured it out. Tell him. Tell him you won the lottery."

"You what?" Ralph asked.

"I *what?*" Harry asked.

"You don't have to pretend anymore. And I don't have to pretend, either. Just tell him you won."

"You won the lottery?" Ralph asked, then gasped. Actually gasped. "You're the mystery lottery winner? Harrison Wells? Thirty-five mil? Good Lord. Another few millions to add to your billions?"

"Your *what?*" Acey asked.

"I didn't win any lottery," Harry said to Acey, then turned to Ralph. "I didn't win anything."

"Your billions?" Acey demanded, her voice nearly a shriek. "What did he mean by that?"

"You don't know who this is?" Ralph asked. "It's pretty early in the morning for you to be here and not know who he is, isn't it?"

"Shut up or I'll shut you up," Harry warned. "Don't talk to her that way."

"What billions?" Acey screamed.

"This here's a billionaire," Ralph said. "Did he forget to mention it?"

"You're…a millionaire," Acey stammered.

"No," Harry said. "I mean, yeah, I am, but not the way you think. I don't know why you thought I won that lottery, but…"

"But I saw the ticket! And then you hid it!"

"No, I didn't." Then Harry appeared to remember something. "Wait, I did buy a ticket for that lottery. For a friend. For a favor. But he didn't win."

"You're a…millionaire anyway?"

"He's heir to a ranching empire," Ralph put in.

"Did I warn you already about shutting up?" Harry asked. "Are you going to do it?"

Ralph shut up.

"It can't be true." Acey's mind was spinning. Harry was rich. All right, that was not news to her. But a different rich. Not newly rich and scared, rather, always rich and…

"I have to sit down," Acey said, somehow getting herself to the sofa. She felt Harry's hand on her elbow to guide her, but she roughly shook it off. As she collapsed, the phone began to ring. Everyone stood there, truth and lies mixed in the air. "It can't be true, it can't be true," Acey kept repeating. "Harry, tell this guy he's wrong. There's some mistake."

The answering machine picked up, and a man's voice, with a drawl as strong as Harry's, began speaking. "Harry, it's Wayne. I just got a phone call from your father this morning, and he says some guy called him at the crack of dawn, some guy from a New York newspaper. He asked your father if he had contact information for you in that town you're in. Your father said no, and told him to piss off, but now your father's calling me, knows you're in New York, wants your number, thinks you're in some kind of trouble. I don't know what's going on there, buddy, but I'm not giving you up. Y'all better straighten this out. Your father the mogul ain't used to people saying no to him and I really don't want him angry at me next."

There was a strange high-pitched sound and Acey realized it was coming from her own throat. She covered her mouth to try to make herself stop.

Wayne's voice went on and on. "He keeps asking if you need money. I told him if you needed money that badly it isn't as if he didn't have billions to spare, but…"

The message eventually stopped and the machine clicked off. Acey stood then. Her legs were shaking hard, but she was determined to be upright for this confrontation. "It is true," she said. "It is."

"Yes," Harry answered.

"Why? Why did you lead me to believe…?"

"That I won the lottery? I didn't do that. I have no idea where that came from."

A rage inside Acey boiled up and bubbled over. "I feel so *stupid!*" she shouted. "Practically right from the beginning, I set out to help you, and it turns out I was just a stupid fool!"

"The only foolish thing I can see is that you thought I won the lottery."

"Someone won," Acey explained, realizing she hadn't been expecting to explain it this way. She had anticipated explaining it with love, with happiness for Harry's luck, instead of surrounded by clouds of misunderstanding. "Someone from the neighborhood. I wanted to know who. I had to know if it was someone…deserving. I asked Rosalia, because the ticket was bought at her store. She said that out of all her regular customers, you were the newest and most…mysterious. It was a long shot, but when I first came here, I saw a ticket on your fridge. I tried to talk to you about the lottery, but you were so weird about money, saying it was terrible and…that's why? Because you have money and you think for some reason that's terrible?"

Harry didn't answer.

"Then," Acey said, "I saw you'd taken the ticket out of my sight after I asked about it. I was sure that the big winner was you and that…you were scared."

"I moved that ticket because I didn't want to look at it. A reminder of so much wealth bugged me."

Acey went on as if she didn't hear. "I did everything I could, as subtly as I could, to make you change your mind about money and accept your windfall. Then, when I started to wonder if maybe I was wrong after all, you gave us money for the cat. I was sure then, but you were rich all along! I'm so stupid! I can't believe you manipulated me like this!"

"Excuse me?" Harry said, raising his own voice. Acey refused to flinch. "*I* manipulated *you?*" he asked. "Is that what you said to me? Because from where I'm standing, it sounds to me a lot like y'all came here, made assumptions, dropped all these hints about '*Don't you think* it would be great to have money?' To convince me to collect some prize you thought I won? While all along, *I* thought *you* were just a hardworking woman who wished she had more, and I busted my butt trying to show you what I've learned, that you don't need money, that you can make your own future. But as it turns out, you were making your own future all along! By manipulating a millionaire into falling in love with you!"

Acey sucked in her breath and actually choked on it. She had to cough a few times and while she did, she had a feeling that if they had been able to sit down and have their truth-telling conversation without interruption, the outcome might very well have been the same. Harry would have accused her, the little pizza girl, of gold-digging.

"Fall in love with me?" Acey asked, her throat still clogged. "I promise you, this is not what I tried to do. I tried not to get…involved like this."

"So did I." Harry's voice was flat.

Tears filled Acey's eyes and she tilted her head back a bit, willing them not to spill over. She might not have a bank account that resembled the one owned by this man, but she had dignity. "Well, I hope this was all fun for you. Because you're not going to be slumming around in *my* backyard anymore."

Harry's face twisted. "Acey, I never, ever, meant for you to think I…"

"Uh, excuse me," Ralph said from the still-open doorway. Acey and Harry whirled to face the forgotten messenger of doom. "Apparently you both had a misunderstanding. And that's not a story for me. Can you just tell me, did you two happen to go riding yesterday?"

Without bothering to figure out the logic that should have accompanied this non-sequitur question, Acey said, "Yes."

"That's all I needed. I have a picture of you guys, and I needed to confirm it was Wells. And your name is…?"

"Get lost," Harry said. "Back into the hall and get out."

"Acey Corelli," Acey said. "That's *a-c-e-y*."

"What are you doing?" Harry demanded.

"Buy yourself a paper tomorrow," Acey said. "Consider our picture your last souvenir of me, of all the fun you had at my expense. In fact," she said, shoving a hand in the front pocket of her jeans and pulling out some change, "it's on me."

She flung two quarters at him, hard, one after another. He caught them both in midair. Then she picked up her bag where she'd dropped it near the door the night before. When they'd fallen into the room together. Before they'd...

Oh, God.

She'd never felt so used, stupid and heartbroken in her life.

She ran to the door, shoved Ralph Wakefield out of the way and bolted.

"I'm sorry, man," Ralph said. "I seem to have contributed to a real mess of things."

Harry pointed to the hallway, and Ralph nodded once politely and left.

Harry sank to his knees and raked his hands through his hair roughly, gripping short strands until his scalp burned. He could only think one thing.

He'd walked away from a fortune, but he'd never lost one. Until now.

Chapter Fourteen

Several days later, when Acey finally climbed out of her bed and rejoined the world, she made an effort to return to her usual life. She went to work, did chores, paid bills, watched Mets games on TV. But it was all soured somehow. The everyday things had lost a luster Acey had never known was even there until the morning it no longer was.

After about a week, she felt she was strong enough to stop into Bread and Milk for some groceries. She needed the strength for Rosalia's inevitable questions.

"Acey!" she cried. "You're here! I've wanted to show you. Look around."

Acey did, and smiled for the first time in many days. Displays were rearranged, there was a box for a weekly and there were other smaller changes that Acey had suggested. She hadn't really known if her ideas were all that viable, considering her lack of experience running a business, but Rosalia clearly thought they were good enough to try.

"It's fantastic," Acey said. "Even better than I imagined."

"You imagined it," Rosalia confirmed. "You are a real businesswoman."

"I don't know about that."

"I sold more comic books this week than any other already. You are a genius. You could run your own store."

Acey had never been the sort of woman to inspire such a compliment, and she blushed now. "That would be something."

"Something you would like?"

"Maybe someday." Acey sighed. Not very long ago, she'd awakened in the arms of her new lover after a night of dreaming about their somedays together.

"How is Harry?" Rosalia asked, demonstrating a little mystical mind reading.

"He's…he's…" Acey choked up. Dammit. And she'd gone two whole hours today without bursting into tears. She thought she was on the road to recovery, but it appeared she was still stuck in the driveway.

"What is it?" Rosalia asked, her face creasing around a frown. She came around the counter to encircle Acey with her arm.

"We broke up."

"You broke up? Which means, you were a couple?"

"For one night only. Then something happened."

"What could happen?"

"He was lying to me."

Rosalia's jaw dropped. "No."

"And I—I wasn't completely honest with him, either, really. It's a big, stinking mess." She sniffled, and Rosalia tore open a miniature packet of tissues for her. Acey blew her nose. "By the way," she said, "you might want to know he didn't win the lottery."

Rosalia raised a brow. "Oh?"

"Nope."

"That can't be why you broke up."

"No, I wouldn't have cared about that. I only cared about him. But he's a…he's a…"

"Rat?"

Acey was startled. "I thought you liked Harry."

"I like Harry. But girlfriends stick together on the same side. No? So, I call him a rat."

"Nah, not rat."

"Snake?"

"I kind of like snakes. He's a…bat."

"A bat?" Now Rosalia looked startled.

"Yeah, a bat. I find bats really vile."

A customer approached the counter with a *TV Guide*. Rosalia eyed him. "Two minutes," she said firmly. "We are having man trouble here."

The customer, a man himself, seemed to decide it prudent not to argue. He flipped through the magazine and waited.

"So you're not talking to Harry the Bat right now?"

"Maybe not ever again." A tear ran down each of Acey's cheeks in a race to her chin.

"That can't be," Rosalia said, rocking her close. "Remember what I said about find the truth and do what your heart tells you?"

"Yes."

"You said he was lying about something. So now you know the whole truth?"

"Yes."

"And your heart, it says what? It says don't talk to Harry ever again?"

"No." Acey stopped. Her heart said run to Harry's house, pound on his door, rip his clothes off, apologize and tell him everything's forgiven. However, her heart was too fragile to combat her more formidable ego, which kept reminding her she'd been made a fool of by another rich man. "I don't know," Acey finally said.

"You are so smart," Rosalia said. "Deep down you know what's good for you. Harry the Bat might still be good for you. Maybe you both start over?"

Acey shook her head. "I don't think so. It would be a risk, and I'm not sure I'm up to getting hurt again."

Rosalia squeezed Acey, then went behind the register and rang up the man's *TV Guide*. When he left, she leaned on her elbows. "I find," she said to Acey, "life is risk. When I moved here and opened my store, it was a risk. Good things happened, like meeting you, and Harry, too. Bad things happened, like once when the store was robbed. And…unexpected things happened. All things that never happened if I didn't take the risk. You see?"

"I see," Acey said. "But I'm still going to just go home and cry for a while."

Rosalia touched Acey's face. "Things will work out for you," she said. "I think you will be surprised. That's what my heart is telling me."

"Dad, it's Harry."

"It's Harrison!" he heard his father echo, no doubt imparting the news to Harry's mother and any employee that might be working nearby. "So," his father said into the mouthpiece. "The prodigal son is heard from once again." The words were stern, but there was a tremor to his voice that Harry couldn't remember ever hearing before.

He was worried about me, Harry realized, and though he felt guilty about having caused that worry, the caring that was behind it motivated Harry to continue.

"Yes, I have. I'm sorry for disappearing."

"Are you all right?" his father asked. "We got calls from a reporter one day, and…"

"It was nothing. He just got pictures of me riding a horse in a park and he wanted to track me down, that's all."

"A horse?" His father sounded understandably flummoxed.

"Yeah, it's a long story, which I'll tell you some other time. I called because I wanted to give you my address and phone number so you and Mom can call me whenever you want. If you want."

"Why the change of mind?" his father asked, then added, "Never mind that. Why did you leave in the first place? Your mother and I could just never understand."

"Dad, the accident really…put me in a bad place."

"We knew that, and you told us you were leaving, but you were so angry at us. When you left, we tried to find out where you went. We asked all your friends, and I even asked your psychologist what was going on. She wouldn't tell me," he said, and Harry was amused at his father's annoyance. Leave it to him to assume that patient confidentiality could be tossed out the window just because he wanted it that way.

Harry sighed. "I was angry. I felt like I had to leave home and money and y'all behind. I really believed that my being rich and privileged was what had ruined me. Turned me into a careless daredevil who didn't care abut anyone's welfare, including my own. And I thought…" Harry took a breath. Might as well admit it now. "I thought you and Mom should have stopped me. That y'all shouldn't have let me keep taking risks, doing my dangerous hobbies."

"You were an adult, Harry," his father reminded him. "We could see you'd decided to be a man of dangerous leisure. We worried about you all the time, but if we had tried to stop you, what would have happened?"

"I would have done whatever I wanted anyway. But listen, I wanted to blame someone or something, and pointing a finger at my upbringing was the easy way out. I didn't understand then that it was wrong, but I understand it now."

"What led to the change of heart?"

"I realized that even after removing myself from my old world, and even after making every effort to help out my fellow man and woman and put myself last, I still somehow managed to screw up and make another big mistake."

Harry heard a sucking sound, and could see in his mind's eye his silvery-haired father, leaning back in his huge chair, smoking a Cuban cigar. "Not to belittle your revelation," he said, "but this sounds suspiciously like woman trouble."

Harry laughed. Even hundreds of miles away, his father had an uncanny ability to read someone. "Yeah, a woman did make me see the light. Before she nearly punched my lights out, that is."

"What are you going to do now?"

Harry took a deep breath, and let it out slowly. "I'm going to stay here," he said. "I'm writing grant proposals."

"No kidding." His father sounded surprised but not displeased.

"Yeah, and I'm not bad at it. In fact, I just found out today I got a nice grant for a no-kill cat shelter. It made me feel really good for the first time since…"

"Since that horse died?"

Harry had been thinking he'd felt good for the first time since Acey left, but knowing that he had helped save shelter cats' lives had healed some of his guilt about Belle and Lara.

"I saw Lara's father recently," his father said. "He said she's doing well. She recently took up riding again."

"I'm really glad. I am."

"Where are you living?"

"In this nice little place right outside the city. I didn't want to be in the middle of everything but I wanted to be near New York. I would love for Mom to fly here and help me decorate. It's been pointed out to me that it's somewhat spartan."

"Have you given up all your hobbies? Hang gliding, rock climbing, parachuting?"

Harry winced. "I think I'm going to retire as king of the X Games," he said. "However, I've found that the opposite, the zero-risk lifestyle, doesn't quite suit me, either. It's time I took a risk again. For the right reason."

"Might this reason have a name?"

"She does," Harry said. "But I'll tell you only if I emerge victorious. The other thing I've learned lately is a big lesson in humility."

He heard a scuffling noise on the other end. "Your mother wants to talk to you," his father said. "Son, if you need anything, anything at all..." His voice trailed off, and Harry knew that what he was trying to say was the first thing Harry's mother said when she came on the line.

"Harry, we love you."

"Love y'all, too."

Harry had one phone call left to make.

"Hello?"

"Hello, Steph. It's Harry."

"Harry, eh? Pretty brave of you to call here."

"I actually called to talk to you."

"If this is one of those get-to-the-girl-by-buttering-up-her-sister moves, it won't work."

"I was wondering how Sherlock is doing."

Steph's protective toughness melted a little, and her voice lost a bit of its edge. "He's okay. The vet took out the tumor and it tested benign. Apparently, it isn't Sherlock's time yet."

Harry was relieved. "That's great."

"Hey, speaking of Sherlock, didn't you get our last three checks?"

"Yes." He'd received a check for twenty dollars from the Corelli sisters every week since he lent them the money. The checks remained in a neat stack on his desk.

"Well, funny, but according to the bank, you haven't cashed any of them yet."

"That's right, and I don't intend to."

"Listen," Steph said. "I understand that you don't exactly need our money, but…"

"I don't want to take your money. You and Acey bust your butts at work to make money and I have no business taking it."

"You're not *taking* it. We *borrowed* it."

"I tried to give it as a gift, and I only gave in and changed it to a loan because Acey didn't know about me and my…"

"Your gigantic piles of dough," Steph said, but not angrily. "Between you and me, I do think you're a nice guy, Harry."

"Thanks."

"I mean it. No matter what Acey's been saying about you."

"And what's that?"

"Oh, why repeat it?" she said in a falsely casual tone. *Great,* Harry thought. "Don't worry," Steph added. "I'm sure she meant it all in the best possible way."

"Oh."

"She's been flagellating herself, too, if it makes you

feel any better. She knows she's at fault. And I must admit I contributed to it myself by encouraging her. Sorry."

"Don't worry about that. It ultimately comes down to the two people involved and, in this case, Acey and I both screwed up big-time."

They were both quiet for a moment. "I want to fix it," Harry said. "I want to fix everything."

"Good luck with that."

"I don't need luck. I need help. That's the other reason I called you."

"Oh, I *knew* it."

"Please, Steph, hear me out," Harry pleaded. When he didn't hear the click of her hanging up on him, he quickly told her his plan.

"Wow," Steph said when he was done. "That's a little crazy, isn't it?"

"Let me tell you what's crazy. What's crazy is that I wake up every morning with an empty space next to me where Acey should be. What's crazy is that I hear her voice in my head but I don't hear it in my ear anymore. What's crazy is that I came so far in my life to find a woman who makes me feel like I can finally be Harry Wells, and I have to be less because I'm not with her. What's crazy is that I love her, and I have a feeling she loves me, and I'm telling *you* that instead of her."

Harry stopped, literally out of breath from the long confession and the accompanying emotions. A few seconds after he had finished, Steph still hadn't spoken.

"Steph?"

"Hang on," Steph said. "I'm writing down all that stuff you just said."

"Not to tell Acey?"

"Hell, no. I'm using this in my manuscript. It's the perfect speech for one of my characters."

"Oh."

"Yeah, he gets bludgeoned to death, so I want to give him something memorable and touching to say before that."

"What do you say, Steph?" Harry asked. "Will y'all help me, you and your boyfriend?"

"I must be out of my mind, but all right," Steph said with a sigh. "On one condition. If this doesn't have the happy ending you're betting on, I'm denying this conversation ever happened."

"I love you, baby."

"I love you, too, sweetie."

Acey rolled her eyes as Lydia and Anthony French-kissed each other over a mound of calzone dough. She never in a thousand years had thought she'd say it, but she wished the lovebirds would perform one of their spectacular, Oscar-deserving fight scenes instead. Acey was far more in the mood for it these days than she was for the recent, almost constant adoration.

Lydia sliced a pie into eight pieces, and Acey remarked, "You and Anthony seem to be getting along better than ever lately."

Lydia stopped midcut, staring behind her at her boyfriend with a dreamy look all over her face. "We made a vow recently to not fight anymore. Even though our love *was* strong enough to survive those silly little things…"

Acey recalled the day Lydia bopped Anthony on the

side of the head with a long loaf of Italian bread because she was convinced he was ogling another woman.

"...we just didn't want to do that anymore."

"Thank God," Steve muttered, placing a pie on the counter and calling, "Large sausage!"

"Oh, you should talk, Mr. Large Sausage," Lydia said. "You and Miss Godzilla inspired the change in the first place."

"Her name is Milla, and everything's just fine with her now, thank you," Steve said. "We've worked it out."

"Worked what out?" Anthony said, coming over to join the conversation. "Did you just call this man Mr. Large Sausage?" he asked Lydia.

"Not for the same reason I call you that," Lydia said.

Anthony kissed her again.

"Get a room," Acey said, smiling a little.

"Nah, we'll just use Lydia's father's office in the back if we have to," Anthony said.

Acey's smile turned into a wince.

"We're all so lucky in love, aren't we?" Lydia asked. "Me and my baby, Steve and veggie-burger girl, and Acey and the Outlaw Cowboy."

"I'm single," Acey said.

Lydia widened her eyes. "Oh, no!" she gasped. "I wondered why you called in sick for a while."

Acey's eyes watered again. Dammit. Every time she was sure she had a firm grip on her emotions.

"Hey," Lydia said, touching her shoulder. "I didn't mean to upset you. Are you all right?"

"No. But he wasn't what I wanted," Acey said firmly.

"That's the important thing. As long as you're absolutely sure of that," Lydia said.

"I am."

"I thought he was a pretty nice guy," Anthony said, and all three of his co-workers gaped at him. Anthony never said anything nice about guys. He considered them all competition. "It's true," he insisted when no one said anything. "I mean, I wouldn't let just anyone come in off the street and try to make time with our Acey. If he needs his ass kicked, I'm happy to do it."

"Permission to hug your boyfriend, please," Acey said to Lydia.

"Permission granted," Lydia said, and Acey hugged Anthony, pressing her cheek to his massive, greasy-apron-covered chest. Lydia threw herself on them and hugged them both. "We love you, Acey," she said. Acey sniffled. Lydia reached an arm out to Steve. "Get over here," she said. "This is a group hug."

"Blecch," Anthony and Steve both said. Steve joined them, but the two men were careful not to touch each other, which made Acey giggle.

"Uh, should we come back another time?" they all heard, and turned to see a group of construction workers standing at the counter, money in their hands, smirking at the emotional outpouring.

"Great," Anthony muttered under his breath. "Only for you, Acey," he said, and went to take their orders.

"It'll be okay," Steve said, patting her back and walking away.

"It will," Lydia confirmed. "You only deserve the best. You're really one in a million, hon."

Acey sighed. Lydia would have been horrified if she understood how her well-intentioned choice of words made Acey's heart ache even more.

"Hey, don't write the order on the pink pad," Lydia said to Anthony. "That's for phone orders. Use the yellow pad."

"What's the difference?" Anthony said.

"Because that's not how it's done."

"And you do everything right all the time?"

Lydia took a deep breath, and Acey smiled a real smile through her tears. Some things just couldn't change, and that was all right.

After her shift, Acey walked the whole way home, thinking again about the things that couldn't change.

When she got home and opened the mail, she was reminded that some things did.

A letter in a plain white envelope congratulated Annamaria Christina Corelli for being chosen to receive a college grant.

Chapter Fifteen

"Aaaceeeyyy!" The sound of Steph's scream echoed around the apartment. "Come quick! Hurry! Get in here!"

In shock, Acey looked up from the bathroom mirror, where she was trying out a new lipstick. Steph's war cry was too déjà vu. Acey remembered the last one, remembered what it had all led to, and her bare feet stuck to the tile floor, refusing to move her.

"Acey! Acey!" Steph called.

"I'm busy!" Acey called back, squeezing her eyes shut.

A jumble of voices tossed around in her memory.

Steph. *One winning ticket. And it was bought at our store.*

Rosalia. *Maybe, you could look at him, tell me if you have the feeling, too?*

Harry. *I want you.*

I want you.

"Acey! Please! Hurry!"

Ignoring the sudden nausea, Acey dropped the lipstick and streaked into the living room. Steph was pointing at the ten-o'clock news on television. Please, Acey prayed, but she had no idea what the rest of it would be. Please what? *Please don't turn my life upside down again.*

She shut her eyes, opened them, and turned to the TV.

Harry.

He was standing there…somewhere…on a bridge. On a bridge? On *the* bridge—the Brooklyn Bridge. "What the hell?" Acey cried.

"Listen!" Steph said sharply.

"…trying to get the attention of the mystery lottery winner," the newscaster was saying. "Harrison Wells, himself a millionaire ranching heir, wouldn't tell reporters why he is pulling this stunt, saying only that his business with the winner is personal."

Acey squinted, but didn't have to. The camera zeroed in on him, standing there, holding up a placard that read in black marker: Mystery Lottery Winner Please Come Forward.

And in smaller black letters under it: (Or I Jump).

"Jump?" Acey gasped, then noticed with some relative relief the huge bungee cord wrapped around his waist.

"Why is he doing this?" Acey asked the television.

"Why are you doing this?" a reporter on TV called to Harry.

"I have my reasons to talk to this person," Harry said. "I promise they're good ones."

"It can't be legal to bungee off that bridge," Steph

said. Acey looked at her sister. "What are you going to do?" Steph asked her. "Just stand there?"

"What am I supposed to do?"

"Acey, do you think it's the lottery winner he really wants to talk to?"

Acey drew a sharp breath in, and it hurt. As much as she was afraid of it, it was clear. Harry wanted her. He knew Steph watched the news every night. He knew Acey would see him.

"I'll wait until midnight," Harry said. A few passersby surrounding him cheered and waved at the camera, which then cut back to the studio.

"Perhaps Wells's stunt will give New York the answer we've all been waiting for," the newswoman said. She looked deep into the camera, deep into Acey's eyes. Acey held her breath. "Where are you?" the woman asked.

"I'm coming," Acey said, grabbed her purse, and dashed out the door.

Acey knew she couldn't stop on the bridge, so she parked Lydia's car a couple of blocks away and walked as fast as she could. After one block, each step began to burn in her lungs, and her eyes began to water with the stress of not being able to walk any faster. She got to the top of the bridge, but there was such a mob in the middle of the walkway that she couldn't get through to Harry.

Suddenly, she felt a hand on her elbow and looked up at Officer Fletch. She poured out her gratitude as he steered her in the bedlam, parting the masses heroically.

"Are you doing this for political reasons?" Acey heard someone yell. Over a sea of heads, she could see it was Ralph Wakefield.

"Now, Ralph," she heard Harry call back, as if he and Ralph were great pals. "I think *you* know what's going on better than that. Like I've said, it's personal."

"How long will you wait?" someone else called.

"Till midnight," Harry said. "Then I'm going down."

A huge cheer went up. Acey felt sick.

Fletch pushed the last person out of her way, and then they were face-to-face.

"Acey!" Harry said, his face lighting up. "What a surprise!"

"You know it's not," she said.

"Is it you?" a woman called to Acey. "Are you the winner?"

"It's not me! Everyone shut up!" Acey yelled.

"I'm glad you're here," Harry said. "Now we can face the lottery winner together when he or she gets here."

"Why? Why are you doing this?"

"Remember when you were so curious about who had won the money, if it was someone who deserved it, that you would do anything to find out?"

"Yes."

"Well, now it's my turn. I want to make sure for myself that this person is the right, deserving person. When he gets here, I'm going to look him in the eye and blame him for everything."

"Everything? What are you talking about?"

"Everything between us. Everything that broke us up."

"Harry, we broke us up. We messed up, and we ruined it."

"Naw, I'm done with that," Harry said. "I've blamed myself for weeks now and I think y'all have, too. I'm done with that now. I want to blame the mystery millionaire for all those problems, and instead concentrate on what we've done *right* for this relationship."

"Har-ry! Har-ry! Har-ry!" a couple of college kids started chanting, and dozens joined in.

A TV camera snapped on near Acey, the white-hot glare nearly blinding her. She put up her arm to shield her face. "Harry, come on down."

"No way. Not until we have a talk about what we've done right."

"Harry, I'm kind of afraid of heights. And bridges. I don't feel so well."

He took her hand. "You'll be fine. I'll go first."

"No, I'll go first. So I can get this over with and get down from here. Listen, I set out to make you happy. Once I determined you were a good man, I set out to make sure you got the prize you deserved. But instead, you gave *me* everything. You reminded me how good life is, no matter how little you have. You saved my cat's life. You saved *my* life. And you showed me I can make a different future for myself, using my brain to achieve things." She looked at him, the breeze ruffling her hair. "I got the grant, Harry."

"You got it?" Harry asked. "Acey! Congrats! I *knew* you would—"

"And," Acey cut him off, "even though I started this whole thing with my good intentions, I ended up giving you nothing!"

"What?" Harry's voice was incredulous. "Acey, look at this. Look at me. You gave me all this."

"Uh..." People danced and chanted and shouted happily at Harry, counting down the minutes to midnight. The bungee harness was a frightening contraption around his torso. "Yeah, great. I gave you all this," Acey said. "The opportunity to stand on the edge of a bridge, threatening to jump, with police waiting to arrest you. Boy, you really got the fine end of this relationship deal."

"What I got," Harry said, "is the chance to be myself. When I left Texas, I left a little too much of myself behind. I came here wanting to start over, but I came here afraid. So afraid."

He reached out and held her chin in his fingers. "I never intended to take a risk again. But you…you made me understand that there are still things in this world worth fighting for, worth taking a chance for. I will do anything for you, Acey Corelli."

Acey grabbed hold of his wrist. She could feel the pulse beneath his skin, and it was speeding up.

"What I'm going to say is the biggest risk of all," Harry said. "Bigger than bungee jumping. But you've allowed me to come this far, so here goes. I love you. Be with me."

He reached into his pocket and pulled out a crumpled scrap of paper. "I found this at home," he said. "If you say no, at least keep this, as a reminder of how you did indeed help me."

Acey took the paper and smoothed it out. His lottery ticket. She looked down at the numbers and wondered why they were so blurry. Then a fat tear plopped onto the paper, and she knew why.

She held the ticket up. "I don't know who won thirty-five million dollars," she said, "and to be honest, I don't care anymore. As far as I'm concerned, *this* ticket is gold. This is the winning ticket. It brought me to you." She wiped her face with the back of her hand. "I love you, Harry."

Harry blinked both eyes hard.

"Ten seconds to midnight!" a man shouted, and the crowd let up a frenzied, New Year's-in-summer-like whoop.

"Harry," Acey said, "I'm about as able to watch you jump off this bridge as I am to jump myself. It will make me throw up. If you want to take a plunge so badly, may I suggest a different kind?"

Harry gave a start. "Are y'all asking me to marry you?"

"You're just leaving me no choice, cowboy," Acey said, then grinned through her tears. "And anyway, it's a pretty good idea. Don't you think?"

When midnight struck, the disappointed crowd shuffled off, booing. Harry and Acey didn't notice or care. They stepped toward each other and kissed, and for that long, blissful moment, their whole world fell away from them. There was no bridge, no city, no lottery, no people. Just Acey and Harry, the luckiest pair who ever lived.

Epilogue

Steph scowled at the mess of wrinkled rose-colored satin bunched up on the ironing board. Sherlock had dragged the dress off the hanger sometime last night and it had to be made presentable before the wedding tomorrow.

She sighed. She'd have to call Ma and ask her how to do this without burning a hole in the fabric.

She glanced at her watch, flipped on the news and tossed her notebook next to the dress. Maybe she'd keep the ironing board out to use as a table. She had a whole lot more space in here now that Acey lived at Harry's place.

Life had changed quickly, Steph mused. After his high-profile Brooklyn Bridge activity, Harry had been brought in by the police for a bit of friendly psychiatric evaluation. Luckily, Harry'd called a doctor back in

Texas willing to vouch for his sanity. Then that *Transcript* reporter, Ralph Wakefield, had written his big story—as the only reporter with the real inside romantic scoop behind Harry's stunt. It was the story New York talked about for one day, which was as long as anyone could get in New York, a city where every day was a new story.

It *was* different not having her sister around, Steph thought. But Acey was overcome with happiness, planning her wedding and her honeymoon safari, so how could Steph complain? Besides, Steph reminded herself, Acey was never any help with ironing anyway.

Steph was trying to smooth one side of the crumpled dress over the board when she heard, "After months of speculation, the mystery thirty-five-million-dollar lottery winner finally came forward today to claim the big prize."

Steph whirled.

There at the lottery office, surrounded by balloons and holding the corner of an oversize cardboard check, was Rosalia.

Steph gasped and screamed, "Oh, my God!" about seven times before she turned up the volume. "…is Rosalia Posada, owner of the Valley Stream convenience store where the ticket was sold," the anchorwoman was saying. "She says she waited to collect so she could get all her affairs settled."

The picture cut to a live shot of Rosalia in the store. Steph could see the cereal display over Rosalia's shoulder, and—her sister? Yep, there was Acey, holding hands with Harry, both beaming bright smiles. Steph rubbed her eyes in disbelief.

"I had many things to do, and to finish up," Rosalia

was saying. "I just needed to take my time. I am sorry for the suspense."

"The whole city *was* wondering about you," the reporter said. "In fact, *this* man—" he gestured to Harry, who waved "—threatened to plunge off the Brooklyn Bridge a few weeks ago because he was desperate to find out your identity."

"Ah," Rosalia said with a sweet smile on her model-beautiful face. She took a step toward Acey and Harry, and they let go of their clasped hands to allow her to stand between them. "My friends are known to do things a bit crazy," Rosalia confided. "But he didn't know it was me. I told him just today."

Acey pulled the microphone towards her. "Steph, don't kill me. I swear we *just* found out about this." The reporter, slightly perturbed, grabbed his mike back. Steph laughed, as did Harry.

"What are your plans?" the reporter asked Rosalia.

"Retire," Rosalia said. "I'm moving to Florida with my family. It's time for me to relax."

"Amen," Steph said.

"I leave the day after tomorrow," Rosalia continued. "I have a wedding to go to first." She squeezed Acey and Harry against her sides.

Light began to creep into Steph's mystery-addicted brain, brightening and brightening until she slapped herself on the forehead. She couldn't believe it took her until the last page of the story to figure it out. Rosalia was the one that planted the Harry idea in Acey's head in the first place. It was Rosalia all along. Acey and Harry were the affair Rosalia needed to settle.

"What about your store?" the reporter asked. "It's a real fixture here in town. Will it close?"

"No," Rosalia said. "With all that's happened, I have not had time to get a wedding gift. So, the store will have to do."

Acey gasped as Rosalia touched her face. "You will do a good job," she told Acey. The two women embraced. Harry kissed the back of Rosalia's head. After a moment, Rosalia untangled herself, remembering her interview. "I know they will love to stay and run it for a long time," she said.

"What a wonderful gesture," the reporter said, sounding a little choked up himself. "Congratulations, Ms. Posada, and to the two new Bread and Milk owners."

"Thank you," they all said, and Steph blew a kiss at the TV. She couldn't wait to see them tomorrow at the wedding.

"Now, let's get reactions from a few of your customers." The reporter turned around. "What do you think of all this?" he asked the nearest person.

Cassandra blinked big, scary eyes out at New York.

"Oh, no," Steph said. "She'll doom us all."

Cassandra began to nod, and kept going like an unstoppable bobble-head doll. She clawed at her black cardigan.

"Ma'am?" the reporter prompted, looking uncomfortable.

Cassandra blinked again. "It is good," she said. And repeated, "It is good."

Steph sighed with relief as the sports news came on.

It was beyond good, she thought as she picked up the phone to call her mother. She hesitated, and dialed her new boyfriend's number instead. The dress could wait a few more minutes.

As Fletch's phone rang, and as she anticipated his

voice, Steph thought, sometimes happy endings truly are the luck of the draw.

Don't you think?

* * * * *

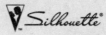

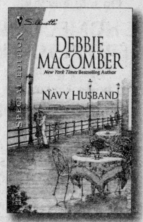

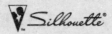

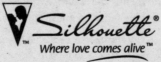